Arthur Wing Pinero

The Schoolmistress

A Farce in Three Acts

Arthur Wing Pinero

The Schoolmistress
A Farce in Three Acts

ISBN/EAN: 9783337401870

Printed in Europe, USA, Canada, Australia, Japan

Cover: Foto ©Andreas Hilbeck / pixelio.de

More available books at **www.hansebooks.com**

THE
SCHOOLMISTRESS

A FARCE
In Three Acts

BY ARTHUR W. PINERO

LONDON   WILLIAM HEINEMANN

MDCCCXCII

INTRODUCTORY NOTE

WHEN, during the season of 1885, the exceptional success of "The Magistrate" had revived the fortunes of the Court Theatre and included that house once again among the popular places of entertainment, the future policy of Messrs. John Clayton and Arthur Cecil's management was practically determined. The essentially comic play, the farce of character and manners, was henceforth to compose the programme, and Mr. Pinero, who had suggested the new policy, and so happily inaugurated it, was naturally commissioned to provide the next play. "The Schoolmistress" was accordingly forthcoming in due time, and in the composition of this piece the author further developed his ideas as to the scope and meaning of modern farce, ideas which will be found briefly expounded in my introductory note to "The Cabinet Minister," published in the present series of Mr. Pinero's plays. "The Schoolmistress" has a very simple stage-history. It was produced at the old Court Theatre on March 27, 1886, and it immediately caught the laughter and applause of the town, the success being so decided that the play retained its place in the programme until January 22, 1887, the total number of performances in the interval having amounted to 290.

For purposes of reference a copy of the "first night programme is here appended :

ROYAL COURT THEATRE.

LESSEES AND MANAGERS,

MR. JOHN CLAYTON AND MR. ARTHUR CECIL.

SATURDAY, MARCH 27, 1886.

THIS EVENING AT HALF-PAST EIGHT O'CLOCK

(FIRST TIME),

THE SCHOOLMISTRESS,

An Original Farce, in Three Acts,

BY

A. W. PINERO.

THE HON. VERE QUECKETT . .	Mr. ARTHUR CECIL.
REAR-ADMIRAL ARCHIBALD RANK-LING, C.B. (H.M. Flag-ship *Pandora*)	Mr. JOHN CLAYTON.
LIEUT. JOHN MALLORY . . .	Mr. F. KERR.
MR. SAUNDERS (Mr. Mallory's nephew, of the Training-ship *Dexterous*) .	Mr. EDWIN VICTOR.
MR. REGINALD PAULOVER . .	Mr. H. EVERSFIELD.
MR. OTTO BERNSTEIN (a Popular Composer)	Mr. CHEVALIER.
TYLER (a Servant)	Mr. W. PHILLIPS.
GOFF	Mr. FRED CAPE.
JAFFRAY	Mr. SUGG.

MRS. RANKLING	Miss EMILY CROSS.
MISS DYOTT (Principal of Volumnia College for Daughters of Gentlemen)	Mrs. JOHN WOOD.
DINAH	Miss CUDMORE.
GWENDOLINE HAWKINS . . .	Miss VINEY.
ERMYNTRUDE JOHNSON . . .	Miss LA COSTE.
PEGGY HESSLERIGGE (an Articled Pupil)	Miss NORREYS.
JANE CHIPMAN	Miss ROCHE.

ACT I.

THE MYSTERY.

Reception Room at Volumnia College, Volumnia House, near Portland Place.

ACT II.

THE PARTY.

Class Room at Volumnia College.

ACT III.

NIGHTMARE.

Morning Room at Admiral Rankling's in Portland Place.

The success in London led to the Court management sending a special company to represent the play in the provinces, where its popularity has been great and enduring, so much so that Mr. Edward Terry has recently added "The Schoolmistress" to his provincial repertoire.

The same story of success must be told of the play's career in Australia and America. Messrs. Brough and Boucicault presented it to the audiences of the Antipodes, where, in the character of Peggy Hesslerigge, Miss Pattie Browne is said to have given a remarkable performance, as the original exponent of the part, Miss Norreys, had done in London. In the United States, Miss Rosina Vokes was responsible for the production of Mr. Pinero's play, but there the principal success was achieved by Mr. Weedon Grossmith in the character of the Hon. Vere Queckett, originally interpreted with so much quaint humour by Mr. Arthur Cecil.

MALCOLM C. SALAMAN.

January 1891.

THE PERSONS OF THE PLAY

THE HON. VERE QUECKETT

MISS DYOTT (Principal of Volumnia College for
    Daughters of Gentlemen)

REAR-ADMIRAL ARCHIBALD RANKLING, C.B. (of
    H.M. Flag-ship *Pandora.*

MRS. RANKLING

DINAH

MR. REGINALD PAULOVER

PEGGY HESSLERIGGE (an Articled Pupil)

LIEUT. JOHN MALLORY (of H.M. Flag-ship
    Pandora)

MR. SAUNDERS (Mr. Mallory's Nephew, of the
    Training-ship *Dexterous*)

GWENDOLINE HAWKINS

ERMYNTRUDE JOHNSON

MR. OTTO BERNSTEIN (a Popular Composer)

TYLER (a Servant)

JANE CHIPMAN

GOFF

JAFFRAY

THE SCHOOLMISTRESS

THE FIRST ACT.

The Scene is the Reception-room at Miss Dyott's *seminary for young ladies, known as Volumnia College, Volumnia House, near Portland Place. The windows look on to the street, and a large door at the further end of the room opens to the hall, where there are some portmanteaus standing, while there is another door on the spectator's right.*

Jane Chipman, *a stout middle-aged servant, and* Tyler, *an unhealthy-looking youth, wearing a page's jacket, enter the room, carrying between them a large travelling-trunk.*

Tyler.

[*Breathlessly.*] 'Old 'ard—'old 'ard! Phew! [*They rest the trunk on the floor,* Tyler *dabs his forehead with a small dirty handkerchief, which he passes on to* Jane.] Excuse me not offering it to you first, Jane.

Jane.

[*Dabbing the palms of her hands.*] Don't name it, Tyler. Do you 'appen to know what time Missus starts?

A

TYLER.

Two-thirty, I 'eard say.

JANE.

It's a queer thing her going away like this alone—not to say nothing of a schoolmistress leaving a lot of foolish young gals for a month or six weeks.

TYLER.

[*Sitting despondently on the trunk.*] Cook and the parlourmaid got rid of too—it's not much of a Christmas vacation we shall get, you and me, Jane.

JANE.

You're right. [*Sitting on the sofa.*] Let's see—how many of our young ladies 'aven't gone home for their 'olidays?

TYLER.

Well, there's Miss 'Awkins.

JANE.

Her people is in India.

TYLER.

Miss Johnson.

JANE.

Her people is in the Divorce Court.

TYLER.

Miss Hesslerigge.

JANE.

Oh, she ain't got no 'ome. She's a orphan, studying for to be a governess.

TYLER.

Then there's this new girl, Miss Ranklin'.

JANE.

Dinah Ranklin'?

TYLER.

Yes, Dinah Ranklin'. Now, why is *she* to spend her Exmas at our College? She's the daughter of Admiral Ranklin', and the Ranklin's live jest round the corner at Collin'wood 'Ouse.

JANE.

Oh, she's been fallin' in love or something, and has got to be locked up.

TYLER.

Well then, last but not least, there's the individual who is kicking his 'eels about the 'ouse, and giving himself the airs of the 'aughty.

JANE.

[*Mysteriously.*] What—Missus's husband?

TYLER.

Yes—Missus's husband.

JANE.

Ah! Mark my word, if ever there was a Mystery, there's one.

TYLER.

Who is he? Missus brings him 'ome about a month ago, and doesn't introduce him to us or to nobody. The order is she's still to be called Miss Dyott, and we don't know even his nasty name.

JANE.

[*Returning to the trunk.*] She calls him Ducky.

TYLER.

Yes, but *we* can't call him Ducky. [*Pointing to the handkerchief which* JANE *has left upon the sofa.*] My 'andkerchief, please. I don't let *anybody* use it.

JANE.

[*Returning the handkerchief.*] Excuse me. [*In putting the handkerchief into his breast-pocket, he first removes a handful of cheap-looking squibs.*] Lor'! You will carry them deadly fireworks about with you, Tyler.

TYLER.

[*Regarding them fondly.*] Fireworks is my only disserpation. There ain't much danger unless anybody lunges at me. [*Producing some dirty crackers from his trousers pockets, and regarding them with gloomy relish.*] Friction is the risk I run.

JANE.

[*Palpitating.*] Oh, don't, Tyler! How can you 'ave such a 'ankering?

TYLER.

[*Intensely.*] It's more than a 'ankering. I love to 'oard 'em and meller 'em. To-day they're damp—to-morrow they're dry. And when the time comes for to let them off——

JANE.

Then they don't go off——

TYLER.

[*Putting the fireworks away.*] P'r'aps not—and it's their 'orrible uncertainty wot I crave after. Lift your end, Jane.

    [*They take up the trunk as* GWENDOLINE HAWKINS *and* ERMYNTRUDE JOHNSON, *two pretty girls, the one gushing, the other haughty in manner, appear in the hall.*

GWENDOLINE.

Here are Miss Dyott's boxes—she is really going to-day. I am so happy!

ERMYNTRUDE.

What an inexpressible relief! Oh, Tyler, I am dissatisfied with the manner in which my shoes are polished.

GWENDOLINE.

Yes—and, Tyler, you never fed my mice last night.

TYLER.

It ain't my place. Birds and mice is Jane's place.

GWENDOLINE.

You are an inhuman boy! [*Shaking* TYLER.]

ERMYNTRUDE.

You are a creature!

JANE.

Don't shake him, Miss, don't shake him!

    [PEGGY HESSLERIGGE *enters through the hall,*

and comes between TYLER *and* GWENDOLINE.
PEGGY *is a shabbily dressed, untidy girl,
with wild hair and inky fingers; her voice
is rather shrewish and her actions are jerky;
altogether she has the appearance of an
overwise and neglected child.*

PEGGY.

Leave the boy alone, Gwendoline Hawkins! What
has he done?

GWENDOLINE.

He won't feed my darling pets.

ERMYNTRUDE.

And he is generally a Lower Order.

PEGGY.

Go away, Tyler. [TYLER *and* JANE *deposit the trunk
in the hall with the other baggage, and disappear.*] You
silly girls! To make an enemy of the boy at the very
moment we depend upon his devotion! It's just like
you, Ermyntrude Johnson!

ERMYNTRUDE.

Don't you threaten me with your inky finger, Miss
Hesslerigge, please.

PEGGY.

Ugh! Haven't we sworn to help Dinah Rankling
with our last breath? Haven't we sworn to free her
from the chains of tyranny and oppression, and never
to eat much till we have seen her safely and happily
by her husband's side!

ERMYNTRUDE.

Yes—but we can't truckle to a pale and stumpy boy, you know.

PEGGY.

We can—we've got to! If Dinah's husband is ever to enter this house we must crouch before the instrument who opens the door—however short, however pasty.

DINAH.

[*Calling outside.*] Are you there, girls?

PEGGY.

[*Jumping, and clapping her hands.*] Here's Dinah!

ERMYNTRUDE *and* GWENDOLINE.

[*Calling.*] Dinah!

> [*They run up to the door to receive and embrace* DINAH, *who enters through the hall.* DINAH *is an exceedingly pretty and simple-looking girl of about sixteen.*

GWENDOLINE.

We've been waiting for you, Dinah.

PEGGY.

And now you're going to keep your promise to us, ain't you?

DINAH.

My promise?

PEGGY.

To tell us all about it from beginning to end,

DINAH.

[*Bashfully.*] Oh, I can't—I don't like to.

PEGGY.

You must ; we've only heard your story in bits.

DINAH.

But where's Miss Dyott ?

PEGGY.

Out—out—out.

DINAH.

And where is *he*—Miss Dyott's husband ?

PEGGY.

What—the Mystery ? [*Skipping across to the left-hand door, and, going down on her knees, peering through the keyhole.*] It's all right. One o'clock in the day, and he's not down yet the imp! I'd cold sponge him if I were Miss Dyott. Places, young ladies. [ERMYNTRUDE *sits with* DINAH *on the sofa,* GWENDOLINE *being at* DINAH's *feet.* PEGGY *perches on the edge of the table, with her feet on a chair.*] H'm ! Now then, Mrs. —— What's your name, Dinah ?

DINAH.

[*Drooping her eyelids.*] Paulover—Mrs. Reginald Paulover.

PEGGY.

Attention for Mrs. Paulover's narrative. Chapter One.

DINAH.

Well, dears, I met him at a party—at Mrs. St.

Dunstan's in the Cromwell Road. He was presented to Mamma and me by Major Padgate.

PEGGY.

Vote of thanks to Major Padgate; I wish *we* knew him, young ladies. Well?

DINAH.

I bowed, of course, and then Mr. Paulover—Mr. Paulover asked me whether I didn't think the evening was rather warm.

PEGGY.

He soon began to rattle on, then. It was his conversation that attracted you, I suppose?

DINAH.

Oh no, love came very gradually. We were introduced at about ten o'clock, and I didn't feel really drawn to him till long after eleven. The next day, being Ma's "At home" day, Major Padgate brought him to tea.

PEGGY.

Young ladies, what is your opinion of Major Padgate?

ERMYNTRUDE.

I think he must be awfully considerate.

DINAH.

He's not—he called my Reginald a "young shaver."

PEGGY.

That's contemptible enough. How old is your Reginald?

DINAH.

He is much my senior he was seventeen in November. Well, the following week Reginald proposed to me in the conservatory. He spoke very sensibly about settling down, and how we were not growing younger; and how he'd seen a house in Park Lane which wasn't to let, but which very likely would be to let some day. And then we went into the drawing-room and told Mamma.

PEGGY, ERMYNTRUDE, *and* GWENDOLINE.

Well, well?

DINAH.

[*Breaking down and putting her handkerchief to her eyes.*] Oh, I shall never forget the scene! I never shall.

PEGGY.

Don't cry, Dinah!

[*They all try to console her.*

DINAH.

Mamma, who is very delicate, went into violent hysterics and tore at the hearthrug with her teeth But a day or two afterwards she grew a little calmer, and promised to write to Papa, who was with his ship at Malta.

PEGGY.

And did she?

DINAH.

Yes. Papa, you know, is Admiral Rankling. His ship, the " Pandora," has never run into anything, and so Papa is a very distinguished man.

GWENDOLINE.

And what was his answer?

DINAH.

He telegraphed home one terrible word—
" Bosh " ! ·

PEGGY, ERMYNTRUDE, *and* GWENDOLINE.

[*Indignantly.*] Oh !

PEGGY.

He ought to be struck into a Flying Dutchman !

DINAH.

The telegraphic rate from Malta necessitates
abruptness, but I can never forgive the choice of
such a phrase. But it decided our fate. Three
weeks ago, when I was supposed to be selecting wools
at Whiteley's, Reginald and I were secretly united at
the Registry Office.

GWENDOLINE.

Oh, how lovely !

ERMYNTRUDE.

How romantic !

DINAH.

We declared we were much older than we really
are, but, as Reginald said, trouble had aged us, so it
wasn't a story. At the doors of the Registry Office
we parted.

ERMYNTRUDE.

How horrible !

GWENDOLINE.

I couldn't have done that !

DINAH.

And when I reached home there was a letter from Papa ordering Mamma to have me locked up at once in a Boarding School; and here I am—torn from my husband, my letters opened by Miss Dyott, quite friendless and alone.

PEGGY.

No, that you're not, Dinah. Listen to me! Miss Dyott is going out of town to-day, and I'm left in charge. I'm a poor governess, but playing jailer over bleeding hearts is not in my articles, and if your husband comes to Volumnia House and demands his wife, he doesn't go away without you—does he, young ladies?

GWENDOLINE *and* ERMYNTRUDE.

No.

PEGGY.

We will do as we would be done by—won't we?

GWENDOLINE *and* ERMYNTRUDE.

Yes!

> [*The street-door bell is heard, the girls cling to each other.*

PEGGY, ERMYNTRUDE, *and* GWENDOLINE.

[*In a whisper.*] Oh!

DINAH.

[*Trembling.*] Miss Dyott!

> [TYLER *is seen crossing the hall.* PEGGY *runs to the window, and looks out.*

PEGGY.

No, it isn't—it's the postman.

DINAH.

A letter from Reginald!

[*TYLER enters with three letters.*

PEGGY.

[*Sweetly.*] Anything for us, Tyler dear ?

TYLER.

[*Looking at the letters, which he guards with one arm.*] One for Miss Dinah Ranklin' !

DINAH.

Oh ! [*Snatching at her letter, which TYLER quickly slips into his pocket.*]

TYLER.

My orders is to hand Miss Ranklin's letters to the missus. [*Handing a letter to PEGGY.*] Miss Hesslerigge.

PEGGY.

[*Surprised.*] For me ?

TYLER.

[*Looking at the third letter.*] Oh, look 'ere, here's a go !

GIRLS.

What's that ?

TYLER.

[*Dancing with delight.*] Oh, crikey ! this must be for *him !*

PEGGY.

Miss Dyott's husband!

GIRLS.

The Mystery!

[*The* GIRLS *gather round* TYLER *and look over his shoulder.*]

PEGGY.

[*Reading the address.*] It's re-addressed from the Junior Amalgamated Club, St. James's Street. [*Snatching the letter from* TYLER.] Gracious! " The Honourable Vere Queckett "!

GWENDOLINE.

The Honourable!

ERMYNTRUDE.

The Honourable!

TYLER.

What's that mean?

PEGGY.

Young ladies, we have been entertaining a swell unawares! [*Returning letter to* TYLER.] Take it up.

TYLER.

Swell or no swell, the person who siles two pairs of boots *per diem* daily is no friend o' mine.

[TYLER *goes out.*

PEGGY.

[*Opening her letter.*] Oh! From Dinah's Reginald!

DINAH.

No, no !

PEGGY.

Addressed to me. [*Referring to the signature.*]
" Reginald Percy Paulover " !

DINAH.

Read it, read it !

> [PEGGY *sits on the sofa, the three girls clustering
> round her :* DINAH *kneeling at her feet
> expectantly.*]

PEGGY.

[*Reading.*] " Montpelier Square, West Brompton.
Dear Miss Hesslerigge,—Heaven will reward you.
The letter wrapped round a stone which you threw
me last night from an upper window of Volumnia
House was handed to me after I had compensated
the person upon whose head it unfortunately
alighted. The news that Dinah has one friend in
Volumnia House enabled me to get a little rest
between half-past five and six this morning."

GWENDOLINE.

One friend !

ERMYNTRUDE.

What about us ?   [DINAH *kisses them.*

DINAH.

Go on !

PEGGY.

[*Reading.*] " Not having closed my eyes for eleven
nights, sleep was of distinct value. Now, dear Miss

Hesslerigge, inform Dinah that our apartments are quite ready——"

GWENDOLINE *and* ERMYNTRUDE.

Oh!

PEGGY.

"And that I shall present myself at Volumnia College, to fetch away the dear love of my heart, to-night at half-past nine." To-night!

GWENDOLINE *and* ERMYNTRUDE.

To-night!

DINAH.

Oh, I've come over so frightened!

PEGGY.

To-night!

> [*Waving the letter and dancing round with delight.*

GWENDOLINE.

Finish the letter.

PEGGY.

[*Resuming her seat, and reading with emotion.*] "Please assure Dinah that I shall love her till death, and that the piano is now moving in. Dinah is my one thought. The former is on the three years' system. Kiss my angel for me. Our carpet is Axminster, and, I regret to say, second-hand. But, oh! our life will be a blessed, blessed dream—the worn part going well under the centre table. This evening at half-past nine. Gratefully yours, Reginald Percy Paulover. P.S.—I shall be closely muffled up, as the corner lamp-post under which I stand is visible from the window of Admiral Rankling's dining-room. You will know me by my faithful, trusty respirator." Oh! I'm so excited! I wish somebody was coming for me!

ERMYNTRUDE.

I know—we shall be frustrated by Jane!

GWENDOLINE.

Or Tyler!

PEGGY.

Leave them to me—I'll manage 'em!

DINAH.

But there's Miss Dyott's husband!

PEGGY.

What? Let the mysterious person who has won Miss Dyott pause before he steps between a young bride and bridegroom! Ladies, Miss Dyott's husband is ours for the holidays. One frown from him and his dinners shall be wrecked, his wine watered, his cigars dampened. He shall find us not girls but Gorgons!

> [*A loud knock and ring are heard at the front door.* JANE *crosses the hall.*

ERMYNTRUDE, GWENDOLINE, *and* DINAH.

[*Under their breath.*] Miss Dyott! Miss Dyott!
> [*They quickly disappear.* PEGGY *remains, hastily concealing the letter.* MISS DYOTT *enters. She is a good-looking, dark woman*

B

of dignified presence and rigid demeanour, her dress and manner being those of the typical schoolmistress.

MISS DYOTT.

Is that Miss Hesslerigge?

PEGGY.

[*Demurely.*] Yes, Miss Dyott.

MISS DYOTT.

How have the young ladies been employing themselves?

PEGGY.

I have been reading aloud to them, Miss Dyott.

MISS DYOTT.

Is Mr. Que—— is my husband down yet?

PEGGY.

I've not had the pleasure of seeing him, Miss Dyott.

MISS DYOTT.

You can join the young ladies, thank you.

PEGGY.

Thank you, Miss Dyott.

[*In the doorway she waves Reginald's letter defiantly, but quickly disappears as* MISS DYOTT *turns round.*

Miss Dyott.

Now, if Vere will only remain upstairs a few moments longer! [*She goes hurriedly to the left-hand door, listens, and turns the key, then to the centre door, listens again and appears satisfied, after which she throws open the window and waves her handkerchief, calling in a loud whisper.*] Mr. Bernstein! Mr. Bernstein! I have left the door on the latch. Come in, please. [*Closing the window and going to the door. Very shortly afterwards,* Otto Bernstein, *a little elderly German, with the air of a musician, enters the room.*] Thank you for following me so quickly. [*Closing the door and turning the key.*]

Bernstein.

You seemed so agitated that I came after your cab mit anoder.

Miss Dyott.

Agitated—yes. Tell me—miserable woman that I am—tell me, what did I sound like at rehearsal this morning?

Bernstein.

Cabital—cabital. Your voice comes out rich and peautiful. Marks my vord—you will make a hit to-night. Have you seen your new name in de pills?

Miss Dyott.

The pills?

Bernstein.

The blay-pills.

Miss Dyott.

I should drop flat on the pavement, if I did.

BERNSTEIN.

It looks very vine. [*Quoting.*] "Miss Constance Delaporte as Queen Honorine, in Otto Bernstein's new Comic Opera, 'Pierrette,' her vurst abbearance in London."

MISS DYOTT.

Oh, how disgraceful!

BERNSTEIN.

Disgraceful! To sing such melodies! No—no, please. Disgraceful! Vy did you appeal to me, dree weeks ago, to put you in the vay of getting through the Christmas vacation?

MISS DYOTT.

[*Tearfully.*] You don't know everything. Sit down! I can trust you. You are my oldest friend, and were a pupil of my late eminent father. Mr. Bernstein, I am no longer a single woman.

BERNSTEIN.

Oh, I am very bleased. I wish you many happy returns of the—eh—no—I congratulate you.

MISS DYOTT.

I am married secretly—secretly, because my husband could never face the world of fashion as the consort of the proprietress of a scholastic establishment. You will gather from this that my husband is a gentleman.

BERNSTEIN.

Il'm—so—is he?

Miss Dyott.

It had been a long-cherished ambition with me, if ever I married, to wed no one but a gentleman. I do not mean a gentleman in a mere parliamentary sense—I mean a man of birth, blood, and breeding. Respect my confidence—I have wedded the Honourable Vere Queckett.

Bernstein.

[*Unconcernedly.*] Ah! Is he a very nice man?

Miss Dyott.

Nice! Mr. Bernstein, you are speaking of a brother of Lord Limehouse!

Bernstein.

Oh, am I? Lord Limehouse—let me tink—he is very—very—vot you gall it?—very popular just now. Yah—yah—he is in the Bankruptcy Court!

Miss Dyott.

[*With pride.*] Certainly. So is Harold Archideckne Queckett, Vere's youngest brother. So is Loftus Martineau Queckett, Vere's cousin. They have always been a very united family. But, dear Mr. Bernstein, you have accidentally probed the one—I won't say fault—the one most remarkable attribute of these great Saxon Quecketts.

Bernstein.

Oh yes, I see; you have to pay your husband's leedle pills.

Miss Dyott.

Quite so—that is it. I have the honour of being

employed in the gradual discharge of liabilities incurred by Mr. Vere Queckett since the year 1876. I am also engaged in the noble task of providing Mr. Queckett with the elaborate necessities of his present existence.

BERNSTEIN.

I know now vy you vanted mine help.

MISS DYOTT.

Ah, yes! Volumnia College is not equal to the grand duty imposed upon it. It is absolutely necessary that I should increase my income. In my despair at facing this genial season I wrote to you.

BERNSTEIN.

Proposing to turn your cabital voice to account, eh?

MISS DYOTT.

Quite so—and suggesting that I should sing in your new Oratorio.

BERNSTEIN.

Well, you are going to do zo.

MISS DYOTT.

What! When you have induced me to figure in a comic opera!

BERNSTEIN.

Yah, yah—but I have told you I have used the music of my new Oratorio for my new Gomic Opera.

MISS DYOTT.

Ah, yes—that is my only consolation.

BERNSTEIN.

Vill your goot gentleman be in the stalls to-night?

MISS DYOTT.

In the stalls—at the theatre! Hush, Mr. Bernstein, it is a secret from Vere. Lest his suspicions should be aroused by my leaving home every evening, I have led him to think that I am visiting a clergyman's wife at Hereford. I shall really be lodging in Henrietta Street, Covent Garden.

BERNSTEIN.

Oh, vy not tell him all about it?

MISS DYOTT.

Nonsense! Vere is a gentleman; he would insist upon attending me to and from the theatre.

BERNSTEIN.

Vell, I should hope so.

MISS DYOTT.

No--no. He is himself a graceful dancer. A common chord of sympathy would naturally be struck between him and the *coryphées*. Oh, there is so much variety in Vere's character.

BERNSTEIN.

Vell, you are a plucky woman; you deserve to be happy zome day.

MISS DYOTT.

Happy! Think of the deception I am practising

upon dear Vere ! Think of the people who believe in the rigid austerity of Caroline Dyott, Principal of Volumnia College. Think of the precious confidence reposed in me by the parents and relations of twenty-seven innocent pupils. Give an average of eight and a half relations to each pupil ; multiply eight and a half by twenty-seven and you approximate the number whose trust I betray this night !

BERNSTEIN.

Yes, but tink of the audience you will delight to-night in my Oratorio—I mean my Gomic Opera. Oh, that reminds me. [*Taking out a written paper from a pocket-book.*] Here are two new verses of the Bolitical Song for you to commit to memory before this evening. They are extremely goot.

MISS DYOTT.

[*Looking at the paper.*] Mr. Bernstein, surely here is a veiled allusion to—yes, I thought so. Oh, the unwarrantable familiarity ! 1 can't—1 can't—even vocally allude to a perfect stranger as the Grand Old Man !

BERNSTEIN.

Oh, now, now—he von't mind dat !

MISS DYOTT.

But the tendency of the chorus—[*reading*] "Doesn't he wish he may get it !" is opposed to my stern political convictions ! Oh, what am I coming to ?

[QUECKETT's *voice is heard.*

QUECKETT.

[*Calling outside.*] Caroline! Caroline!

MISS DYOTT.

Here's Vere! [*Hurriedly to* BERNSTEIN.] Good-bye, dear Mr. Bernstein—you understand why I cannot present you.

BERNSTEIN.

[*Bustling.*] Good-bye—till to-night. Marks my vord, you vill make a great hit.

QUECKETT.

[*Calling.*] Caroline!

MISS DYOTT.

[*Unlocking the centre door.*] Go—let yourself out.

BERNSTEIN.

Goot luck to you!

MISS DYOTT.

[*Opening the door.*] Yes, yes.

BERNSTEIN.

And success to my new Oratorio—I mean my Gomic Opera.

MISS DYOTT.

Oh, go!

> [*She pushes him out and closes the door, leaning against it faintly.*

QUECKETT.

[*Rattling the other door.*] I say, Caroline!

Miss Dyott.

[*Calling to him.*] Is that my darling Vere?

QUECKETT.

[*Outside.*] Yes.

[*She comes to the other door, unlocks and opens it.* VERE QUECKETT *enters.* He is a fresh, breezy, dapper little gentleman of about forty-five, with fair curly hair, a small waxed moustache, and a simple boyish manner. He is dressed in the height of fashion and wears a flower in his coat, and an eye-glass.*]

QUECKETT.

Good morning, Caroline, good morning.

Miss Dyott.

How is my little pet to-day? [*Kissing his cheek, which he turns to her for the purpose.*] Naughty Vere is down later than usual.

QUECKETT.

It isn't my fault, dear; the florist was late in sending my flower.

Miss Dyott.

What a shame!

QUECKETT.

[*Shaking out a folded silk handkerchief.*] Oh, by the bye, Carrie, I want some fresh perfume in my bottles.

Miss Dyott.

My Vere shall have it.

Queckett.

Thank you—thank you. [*Sitting before the fire, opening the newspaper, and humming a tune.*] Let me see—let me see. Ah, here we are—"Court of Bankruptcy—before the Official Receiver." Limehouse came up again for hearing yesterday. How they bother him! They bothered me in '75. Now, here's a coincidence, Carrie. In 1875 my assets were *nil*—in 1885 dear old Bob's assets are *nil*. Now that's deuced funny.

Miss Dyott.

Vere, dear, have you forgotten what to-day is?

Queckett.

[*Referring to the head of paper.*] December the twenty-second.

Miss Dyott.

Yes, but it's the day on which I am to quit my Verey.

Queckett.

Oh, you've stuck to going, then! Well, I daresay you're right, you know. You've a very bad cold. Nothing like change for a bad cold—change of scene, change of pocket-handkerchiefs, and so on.

Miss Dyott.

But you don't say anything about your own

lonely Christmas. I have married a man who is too unselfish.

> [*The centre door opens slightly, and the heads of the three girls, PEGGY, GWENDOLINE, and ERMYNTRUDE appear one above the other, spying.*]

QUECKETT.

[*Putting down his paper.*] Lonely? By Jove, these inquisitive pupils of yours won't let a fellow be lonely! Upon my soul, they are vexing girls.

MISS DYOTT.

But they are a source of income, dear.

QUECKETT.

They are a source of annoyance. I've never had the measles—I've half a mind to catch it and give it to 'em. Now if I could only while away my evenings somewhere, these vexing girls wouldn't so much matter. [*He rises, the heads disappear, and the door closes. Listening.*] What was that?

MISS DYOTT.

The front door, I think.

QUECKETT.

I thought it might be those vexing girls—they're always prying about. I was going to say, Carrie, why not let me withdraw my resignation at the Junior Amalgamated Club and continue my membership?

Miss Dyott.

Ten guineas a year for such an object I cannot afford, and will not pay, Vere.

Queckett.

Upon my soul, I might just as well be nobody, the way I'm treated.

Miss Dyott.

Oh, my king, don't say that! Have you thought about the Christmas expenses?

Queckett.

Frankly, my dear, I have not.

Miss Dyott.

Have you forgotten that my rent is due on Friday?

Queckett.

Completely.

Miss Dyott.

And then think—only think of your boots!

Queckett.

Oh, dash it all—what man of any position ever thinks of his boots? [*Producing a leteer.*] The fact is, Caroline, I have had a note—sent on to me from the club—from my friend, Jack Mallory. He is first lieutenant on the "Pandora," you know, and just home after four years at Malta. He reached London yesterday, and writes me—[*Reading*] "Now, old chap, do let's have one of our old rollicking nights together, and——"

Miss Dyott.

What!

Queckett.

Eh? [*Correcting himself.*] He writes me—[*Referring to the letter.*] "Now, old chap, do let me give you the details of our new self-loading eighty-ton gun." Well, Carrie, what the deuce am I to do? It seems a nice gun. [*She shrugs her shoulders.*] Carrie, what is your Vere to do? [*She makes no answer, he approaches her and touches her on the shoulder.*] Carrie. Carrie, look at your Vere. Vere speaks to you. [*He sits on her lap, she looks up affectionately.*] Carrie, darling, you know old Jack is such a devil——

Miss Dyott.

Eh?

Queckett.

A nice devil, you know—an exceedingly nice devil. Now I can't show up at the Club after sending in my resignation—they'd quiz me awfully. But I must entertain poor old Jack. [*Coaxingly.*] Eh? Resignation sent in through misunderstanding, eh? [*Pinching her cheek.*] Ten little ginny-winnies, eh?

Miss Dyott.

Not a ginny-winny! For a Club, not half a ginny-winny!

Queckett.

Caroline, you forget what is due to me.

Miss Dyott.

I wish I could forget what is due to everybody.

Don't be cross, Vere. I'll fetch your hat and coat, and Vere shall go out for his little morning stroll. And if he promises not to be angry with his Caroline, there are five shillings to spend.

[*She gives him some silver ; he looks up beamingly again.*

QUECKETT.

My darling !

MISS DYOTT.

[*Taking his face between her hands, and kissing him.*] Um—you spoilt boy !

[*She runs out.*

QUECKETT.

Now what am I to do about Jack? I can't ask him here. Carrie would never allow it, and if she would I couldn't stand the chaff about marrying a Boarding School. No, I can't ask Jack here. *Why* can't I ask Jack here? Everybody in bed at nine o'clock—square the boy Tyler to wait. Bachelor lodgings, near Portland Place. Extremely good address. Jack *shall* give me the details of that eighty-ton gun. Yes—and we'll load it, too. While I'm out I'll send this wire to Jack.

QUECKETT.

[*Taking a telegraph form from the stationery-cabinet, and writing.*] "Come up to-night, dear old boy. Nine-thirty sharp. Diggings of humble bachelor. 8o, Duke Street, Portland Place. Bring two or three good

fellows.—Vere." How much does that come to?
[*Counting the words rapidly.*] One—two—three—four
—five—no. [*Getting confused.*] One—two—three—
four—five—six—no. One—two—three—four—five
—six. [*Counting to the end.*] I think it is one and
something halfpenny—but it's all luck under the new
regulations. Oh, and I haven't addressed it! Where's
Jack's letter?

> [*He takes the letter from his pocket.* PEGGY
> *enters quietly. Seeing* QUECKETT, *she draws
> back, watching him.*

PEGGY.

[*To herself.*] What is he doing now—the Guy
Fawkes?

QUECKETT.

[*Referring to the letter.*] Ah, "Rovers' Club"! [*Addressing the telegram.*] "John Mallory, Rovers' Club."
Let me see—that's in Green Street, Piccadilly. [*Writing.*] "Green Street, Piccadilly." Or am I thinking
of the "Stragglers'"? I've a Club list upstairs—I'll
go and look at it. [*Humming an air, he shuts up the
telegraph form in the blotting-book, and rises, still with
his back to* PEGGY.] I feel so happy!

> [*He goes out.*

PEGGY.

[*Advances to the blotting-book, carrying some luggage
labels.*] Miss Dyott has sent me to address her
luggage labels. I am compelled to open that blotting-book. [*She sits on the chair lately vacated by*
QUECKETT, *and opens the blotting-book mischievously
with her forefinger and thumb. Seeing the telegraph*

form.] Ah ! [*Reading it greedily with exclamations.*]
Oh ! " Dear old boy ! " Oh ! " Diggings of humble
bachelor ! " Oh ! " Bring two or three good
fellows ! " Oh-oh ! [*Sticking the telegraph form promi-
nently against the stationery cabinet, facing her, and
addressing a luggage label.*] " Miss Dyott, passenger
to Hereford."

QUECKETT.

[*Re-entering gaily.*] It *is* in Green Street, Piccadilly.

> [*He sees* PEGGY, *and stands perplexed,
> twisting his little moustache.*

PEGGY.

[*Writing solemnly.*] " Miss Dyott, passenger to
Hereford."

QUECKETT.

[*Coughing anxiously.*] H'm ! I fancy I left an
eighty-ton gun—I mean, I think I've mislaid a—
er—— [*Without looking up,* PEGGY *re-adjusts the
telegraph form against the cabinet.*] Oh ! H'm ! That's
it. [*He makes one or two fidgety attempts to take it,
when* PEGGY *rises with it in her hand. She reads it
silently, forming the words with her lips.*] Oh, you
vexing girl! What do you think of doing about
it ? [*She commences to fold the form very neatly.*] You
know I sha'n't send it. I never meant to send it. I
say, I shall not send it. [*Nervously holding out his
hand.*] Shall I ? [PEGGY *doubles up the form into
another fold without speaking.*] You *are* a vexing
girl.

MISS DYOTT.

[*Calling outside.*] Miss Hesslerigge !

[PEGGY *quietly slips the telegraph form into her pocket.*

QUECKETT.

Oh! You won't tell my wife! You will not *dare* to tell my wife! [*Mildly.*] Will you?

MISS DYOTT.

[*Calling again.*] Miss Hesslerigge!

QUECKETT.

[*In agony.*] Oh! [*Between his teeth.*] Do you—do you know any bad language?

PEGGY.

I went to the Lord Mayor's Show once; I heard a little.

QUECKETT.

Then I regret to say I use it to you, Miss Hesslerigge —I use it to you!

[MISS DYOTT *enters, carrying* QUECKETT's *hat, gloves, and overcoat.*

MISS DYOTT.

You can address the labels in another room, Miss Hesslerigge, please.

QUECKETT.

[*To himself.*] Will she tell?

PEGGY.

[*To herself.*] He is in our power!

[PEGGY *goes out.*

Miss Dyott.

[*Putting the hat on* Queckett's *head.*] You look sickly, my Vere.

Queckett.

I shall be better after my stroll, Caroline.

[*A knock and ring are heard.*

Miss Dyott.

[*Assisting* Queckett *with his overcoat.*] As you have some solitary evenings before you, you may lay in a few cigars, Vere darling.

Queckett.

Thank you, Carrie.

Miss Dyott.

[*Helping him to put on his gloves like a child.*] But, for the sake of our depressed native industries, I beg that you will order those of purely British origin and manufacture. [TYLER *enters carrying a large common black tea-tray upon which is a solitary visiting-card.*] Where's the salver, you bad boy!

Tyler.

[*Pointing to* Queckett, *sullenly.*] 'E slopped his choc'late over it.

Miss Dyott.

[*Taking the card.*] Admiral and Mrs. Rankling— Dinah's parents! I must see them.

Queckett.

[*Hastily turning up his collar to conceal his face.*]

No, no! They know me—they are old friends of my family's!

> [*TYLER shows in* ADMIRAL *and* MRS. RANK-
> LING. MRS. RANKLING *is a thin, weak-look-
> ing, faded lady with a pale face and anxious
> eyes. She is dressed in too many colours,
> and nothing seems to fit very well. AD-
> MIRAL RANKLING is a stout, fine old gentle-
> man with short crisp grey hair and fierce
> black eyebrows. He appears to be suffering
> inwardly from intense anger.*

MISS DYOTT.

My dear Mrs. Rankling.

> [*The ladies shake hands.* TYLER *goes out.*

MRS. RANKLING.

[*Pointing to* RANKLING.] This is Admiral Rankling.

> [MISS DYOTT *bows ceremoniously.* RANKLING
> *returns a slight bow and glares at her.*

MISS DYOTT.

[*To* MRS. RANKLING.] Pray sit by the fire.

> [*As the ladies move to the fire,* QUECKETT, *who
> has been watching his opportunity, creeps
> round at the back and goes out.*

MRS. RANKLING.

[*Warming her feet at the fire.*] The Admiral has called upon you, Miss Dyott, with reference to our child, Dinah.

[RANKLING, *with a smothered exclamation of rage, sits on the sofa.*

MISS DYOTT.

Whom we find the charming daughter of charming parents..

    [RANKLING *gives her a fierce look, which frightens* MISS DYOTT, *who is most anxious to conciliate the* ADMIRAL.

MRS. RANKLING.

Dinah's obstinacy is a very serious shock to the Admiral, who is naturally unused to insubordination.

MISS DYOTT.

Naturally.

    [RANKLING *glares at her again ; she puts her hand to her heart.*

MRS. RANKLING.

The Admiral has been stationed with his ship at Malta for a long period—in fact the Admiral has not brightened our home for over four years.

MISS DYOTT.

How more than delightful to have him with you again !

    [RANKLING *gives* MISS DYOTT *a fearful look ; she clutches her chair.*

MRS. RANKLING.

The Admiral has one of those fine English tempers

—generous but impetuous. You may guess the sad impression Dinah's ingratitude has produced upon him. It is an open secret that the Admiral made three wills yesterday, and read King Lear's curse after supper in place of Thanksgiving.

RANKLING.

[*Sharply.*] Emma!

MRS. RANKLING.

[*Starting.*] Yes, Archibald.

RANKLING.

Leave the fire—you'll be chilled when we go. Come over here.

MRS. RANKLING.

Yes, Archibald.

[*Crossing the room in a flutter and sitting beside* RANKLING, *who makes insufficient room for her.*

MRS. RANKLING.

Thank you, Archibald. I have been sitting up with the Admiral all night, and it is owing to my entreaties that he has consented to give Dinah one last chance of reconciliation.

RANKLING.

[*Who has been eyeing her.*] Emma!

MRS. RANKLING.

Yes, Archibald.

RANKLING.

Your bonnet's on one side again.

MRS. RANKLING.

[*Adjusting it.*] Thank you, Archibald. We leave town for the holidays to-morrow; it rests with Dinah whether she spends Christmas in her papa's society or not.

RANKLING.

Don't twitch your fingers, Emma—don't twitch your fingers.

MRS. RANKLING.

[*Nervously.*] It's a habit, Archibald.

RANKLING.

It's a very bad one.

MRS. RANKLING.

All we require is that Dinah should personally assure us that she has banished every thought of the foolish young gentleman she met at Mrs. St. Dunstan's.

MISS DYOTT.

[*Rising and ringing the bell.*] If I am any student of the passing fancies of a young girl's mind——

RANKLING.

Speak louder, ma'am—your voice doesn't travel.

MISS DYOTT.

[*Nervously—with a gulp.*] If I am any student of

the passing—fancies — [RANKLING *puts his hand to his ear.*] Oh, don't make me so nervous.

> [JANE *enters, looking untidy, her sleeves turned up, and wiping her hands on her apron.*

MISS DYOTT.

[*Shocked.*] Where is the man-servant?

JANE.

On a herring, ma'am.

MISS DYOTT.

Ask Miss Dinah Rankling to be good enough to step down-stairs.

> [JANE *goes out.* RANKLING *rises, with* MRS. RANKLING *clinging to his arm.*

MRS. RANKLING.

You will be calm, Archibald—you will be moderate in tone. [*With a little nervous cough.*] Oh, dear! poor Dinah!

RANKLING.

Stop that fidgety cough, Emma.

> [*Stalking about the room, his wife following him.*

MRS. RANKLING.

Even love-matches are sometimes very happy. Ours was a love-match, Archibald.

RANKLING.

Be quiet—we're exceptions.

[*Pacing up to the door just as it opens, and*
PEGGY *presents herself. Directly* RANK-
LING *sees* PEGGY, *he catches her by the*
shoulders, and gives her a good shaking.

MISS DYOTT.

Admiral !

MRS. RANKLING.

Archibald !

PEGGY.

[*Being shaken*] Oh—oh—oh—oh !

RANKLING.

[*Panting, and releasing* PEGGY] You good-for-
nothing girl ! Do you know you have upset your
mother ?

MRS. RANKLING.

Archibald, that isn't Dinah !

MISS DYOTT.

That is another young lady.

RANKLING.

[*Aghast.*] What—not—— Who—who has led me
into this unpardonable error of judgment ?

MRS. RANKLING.

[*To* PEGGY, *who is rubbing her shoulders and looking*
vindictively at RANKLING.] Oh, my dear young lady,
pray think of this only as an amusing mistake. The
Admiral has been away for more than four years—
Dinah was but a child when he last saw her. [*Weeping.*]
Oh, dear me !

Rankling.

Be quiet, Emma—you'll make a scene.

Miss Dyott.

[*To* Peggy.] Where is Miss Rankling?

Peggy.

Miss Rankling presents her compliments to Miss Dyott, and her love to her papa and mamma, and, as her mind is quite made up, she would rather not cause distress by granting an interview.

[Rankling *sinks into a chair.*

Mrs. Rankling.

Archibald!

Miss Dyott.

[*To* Peggy.] The port wine!

[Peggy *advances with the cake and wine.*

Mrs. Rankling.

[*Kneeling to* Rankling.] Archibald, be yourself! Remember, you have to respond for the Navy at a banquet to-night. Think of your reputation as a genial after-dinner speaker!

Rankling.

[*Rising with forced calmness.*] Thank you, Emma. [*To* Miss Dyott.] Madam, my daughter is in your charge till you receive instructions from my solicitor. [*Glaring at* Peggy.] A short written apology shall be

sent to this young lady in the course of the afternoon.
[*To his wife.*] Emma, your hair's rough—come home.

> [*He gives* Mrs. Rankling *his arm. They
> go out.* Miss Dyott *sinks exhausted on
> sofa.* Peggy *offers her a glass of wine.*

Miss Dyott.

Oh, my goodness! [*Declining the wine*] No, no—
not that. It has been decanted since Midsummer.

> [Queckett, *his coat collar turned up, appears
> at the door, looking back over his shoulder.*

Queckett.

What's the matter with the Ranklings? [*Seeing*
Miss Dyott *and* Peggy] Oh! has that vexing girl
told Caroline?   [*The clock strikes two.*

Miss Dyott.

[*To herself.*] Two o'clock—I must remove to Henrietta Street. [*Seeing* Queckett.] My darling.

Queckett.

My love. [*To himself.*] All right.

Miss Dyott.

I am going to prepare for my journey—the train
leaves Paddington at three.

> [*As* Miss Dyott *goes towards the centre door,*
> Jane *enters carrying about twenty boxes
> of cigars, which she deposits on the floor
> and then goes out.*

Miss Dyott.

What is this?

Queckett.

H'm ! my cigars, Carrie—brought 'em with me in a cab.

Miss Dyott.

Oh ! [*Reading the label of one of the boxes.*] " Por Carolina." Ah, poor Caroline.

> [*She goes out. Directly she is gone,* Peggy *and* Queckett, *by a simultaneous movement, rush to the two doors and close them.*

Queckett.

Now, Miss Hesslerigge !

Peggy.

Sir.

Queckett.

We will come to a distinct understanding.

Peggy.

If you please.

Queckett.

In the first place, you will return me my telegram.

Peggy.

I can't.

Queckett.

You mean you won't.

Peggy.

No, I can't.

QUECKETT.

Why not?

PEGGY.

I have just sent it to the telegraph office by Tyler.

QUECKETT.

Despatched it!

PEGGY.

Despatched it—it was one and fourpence.

QUECKETT.

Oh, you—you—you vexing girl! Mr. Mallory will be here to-night.

PEGGY.

Yes—and will " Bring two or three good fellows." At least we hope so.

QUECKETT.

Hope so!

PEGGY.

[*Standing over him with her arms folded.*] Listen, Mr. Vere Queckett. [*He starts.*] We ladies are going to give a little party to-night to celebrate a serious event in the life of one of us. We have invited only one young gentleman; your friends will be welcome.

QUECKETT.

Oh!

PEGGY.

Without us your party must fail, for we command the servants. Let it be a compact—your soirée shall be our soirée, and our soirée your soirée.

QUECKETT.

And if I indignantly decline?

PEGGY.

[*Solemnly.*] Consider, Mr. Queckett—your Christmas holidays are to be passed with us. Think in which direction your comfort and freedom lie—in friendship or in enmity? Even now, Ermyntrude Johnson is trimming the holly with one of your razors.

QUECKETT.

But what explanation could I give Mr. Mallory of your presence here?

PEGGY.

Every detail has been considered. You are our bachelor uncle.

QUECKETT.

Uncle!

PEGGY.

We are your four nieces.

> [QUECKETT *looks up—is tickled by the idea,*
> *and bursts out laughing.* PEGGY *joins.*

QUECKETT.

I don't see why that shouldn't be rather jolly.

PEGGY.

[*Roguishly.*] D'ye consent?

QUECKETT.

Can't help myself—can I?

PEGGY.

[*Delighted.*] That you can't.

QUECKETT.

Let's be friends, then—shall we? Have you girls got any money?

PEGGY.

No. Have you?

QUECKETT.

No! that is, all mine's invested.

MISS DYOTT.

[*Outside.*] Tyler, fetch a cab. [QUECKETT *makes a bolt from the room, and* PEGGY *rigorously re-arranges the furniture as* MISS DYOTT *enters, dressed as if for a journey, and carrying her umbrella and hand-bag again.*] Where is my husband?

PEGGY.

[*Looking about her.*] Your hand-bag, Miss Dyott?

[QUECKETT *re-enters.*

MISS DYOTT.

Still in your overcoat, dear?

QUECKETT.

Of course, Carrie. I'll drive with you to Paddington.

Miss Dyott.

No, no—I insist on going alone.

Queckett.

[*Taking off his coat with alacrity.*] Oh, Carrie, I *am* disappointed !

> [Dinah, Gwendoline, *and* Ermyntrude *come through the hall into the room, and form a group.* Jane *enters the hall.* Tyler *joins her there.*

Miss Dyott.

Miss Hesslerigge—young ladies. I regret to say I am compelled to—to quit Volumnia House for a time. The length of my absence depends upon how long it runs—[*correcting herself in confusion*]—upon how long it runs to it, to employ a colloquialism of the vulgar. But I depart with a light heart, because I leave my husband in authority. He will find a trusty lieutenant in Miss Hesslerigge. Ladies, to abandon for the moment our mother tongue, *Je vous embrasse de tout mon cœur—soyez sages !*

Girls.

[*Together.*] *Au revoir, Mademoiselle Dyott ! Bon voyage, Mademoiselle Dyott !*

> [Peggy *joins the Girls and they talk earnestly. A Cabman is seen carrying out the boxes from the hall, assisted by* Tyler. Miss Dyott *produces some paper packets of money from her hand-bag.*

Miss Dyott.

[*As she gives the packets to* Queckett.] Vere, the house-agent will apply for the rent—there it is. Our fire insurance expired yesterday—post the premium to the Eagle Office at once. Jane's wages are due next week—deduct for the broken water-bottle. When you need exercise, dear one, tidy up the back yard—the recreation ground. A charwoman assists Jane on Fridays—three-quarters of a day, and leaves before her tea. Good-bye, Vere.

Tyler.

The cab's a-waitin', ma'am.

[Miss Dyott *takes* Queckett's *arm*.

The Girls.

Good-bye, Miss Dyott.

[Miss Dyott *and* Queckett *go out through the hall*. Peggy, Ermyntrude, *and* Gwendoline *run over to the windows and look out*. Dinah *sits apart, thinking*.

Ermyntrude.

There they are !

Gwendoline.

Miss Dyott's in the cab !

Peggy.

She's off !

The Three.

Hurrah ! Hurrah !

D

[QUECKETT *returns, the* GIRLS *surround him demonstratively.*

PEGGY.

Dinah—young ladies—[*pointing to* QUECKETT]—Uncle Vere!

ERMYNTRUDE *and* GWENDOLINE.
[*Together.*] Uncle Vere!   Uncle Vere!

[QUECKETT *tries to maintain his dignity, and pushes the girls from him.* TYLER, *with* JANE, *is seen letting off a squib in the hall.*

END OF THE FIRST ACT.

THE SECOND ACT

The Scene is a plain-looking School-room at MISS DYOTT'S. *Outside the two windows runs a narrow balcony, and beyond are seen the upper stories and roofs of the opposite houses. There are two doors facing each other. The room is decorated for the occasion with holly and evergreen, and a table is laid with supper:*

PEGGY *is standing on a chair, with a large hammer in her hand, nailing up holly.*

PEGGY.

[*Surveying her work.*] There! I'm sure Miss Dyott wouldn't recognise the dull old class-rooms. [*Descending.*] I think it's time I dressed. [QUECKETT *enters slowly ; he is in a perfectly-fitting evening dress, with a flower in his button-hole, but looks much depressed. He and* PEGGY *regard each other for a moment silently.*] Oh, I'm so glad you're ready early ! How good it makes one feel, giving pleasure to others —doesn't it ? Aren't you well ?

QUECKETT.

Yes—no. I deeply regret plunging into the vortex of these festivities.

PEGGY.

Oh, I suppose you're nervous in society.

QUECKETT.

[*Drawing himself up.*] Nervous in society, Miss Hesslerigge?

PEGGY.

What do you think of the decorations? Artistic, aren't they?

QUECKETT.

A treat at a Sunday School!

PEGGY.

Then you shouldn't have locked up the rooms downstairs.

QUECKETT.

I daren't allow the neighbours to see the house lighted up downstairs. I wish I could have locked up all you vexing girls.

PEGGY.

That's not the spirit to give a party in! [*Contemplating the table.*] How many do you think your friend, Mr. Mallory, will bring?

QUECKETT.

I don't think Mr. Mallory will find his way here at all. Have you observed the fog?

PEGGY.

Is it foggy?

QUECKETT.

You can't see your hand before you outside.   I
sincerely hope my friend will *not* come.

PEGGY.

There's hospitality!   Ours will.

QUECKETT.

Who *is* your friend?

PEGGY.

Mr. Paulover.

QUECKETT.

And who the devil is——

PEGGY.

I don't think that's the language for a party, Mr.
Queckett!

QUECKETT.

I beg your pardon.   Who is Paulover?   [TYLER
*enters with a bill in his hand, with his hair stiffly
brushed and greased, and wearing an expression of
intense wonderment.*]   What's this?

TYLER.

A beautiful large lobster salid is come, sir.

QUECKETT.

[*Looking at* PEGGY.]   *I* haven't ordered a lobster
salad.   [*In an undertone.*]   You know, this is getting
extremely vexing.   [*He takes from his pocket the packets
of money previously given him by* MISS DYOTT.]   I've

already paid a bill for some oysters and a *pâté de foie
gras.*   Jane's wages went for that. [*Opening a
packet.*] Now, here's a salad.   That breaks into next
week's household expenses. [*Handing the money to*
TYLER, *who goes out.*]

PEGGY.

We're only girls, you know.   And you seem to
forget you're our uncle.

QUECKETT.

[*Irritably.*] I am *not* your uncle.

PEGGY.

To-night you are.   But you needn't be our uncle
to-morrow.

QUECKETT.

[*Gloomily.*] Somebody will have to be *my* uncle to-
morrow.   Then I understand there's a lark pudding
ordered for half-past nine.   I can't allow the account
to be sent in to—to——

PEGGY.

To Auntie?

QUECKETT.

Well—to—to Auntie.   Who pays for the lark
pudding?

PEGGY.

You couldn't well ask girls to do it; besides, it's
your party.

QUECKETT.

It is *not* my party, and it is *your* lark pudding.

PEGGY.

It may be our lark—but it's your pudding.

> [TYLER *enters, still much astonished, and with another bill.*

QUECKETT.

[*Taking the bill.*] What's that?

TYLER.

Sich a lot of champagne's come, sir!

PEGGY.

Champagne! Who ordered that? *I* didn't.

QUECKETT.

Hush! I did—I did—I did.

PEGGY.

Then it *is* your party?

QUECKETT.

Part of the party is my party. [*Opening another packet.*] I've broken into the rent. [*He hands* TYLER *the bill and some money, pocketing the remainder.* TYLER *goes out.*] The Fire Insurance alone remains intact. [*Opening the last packet.*] Postal Orders for thirty shillings. I'll despatch that, at any rate. [*He sits at the writing-table and begins to write.* PEGGY *hammers* up *the last piece of holly as* QUECKETT *tries to write.*] Oh, you vexing girl!

PEGGY.

Beg pardon ; this is the last blow.

> [*She gives another knock as* JANE *enters, carrying a large ornamental wedding-cake.* JANE *is in a black gown and smart cap and apron ; her eyes are wide open with pleasure and astonishment.* JANE *deposits the cake upon the writing-table before* QUECKETT.

JANE.

'Scuse me, sir ; the confectioner's jest brought the things.

QUECKETT.

What's that ? *That* isn't the lark pudding.

JANE.

Oh, lor', no, sir !   [*She goes out.*

PEGGY.

Oh, that's the wedding-cake.

QUECKETT.

Oh, come—it isn't my wedding-cake.

PEGGY.

[*Laughing.*] Oh, don't, you funny man ! No, it's Mr. Paulover's.

QUECKETT.

Who the dev——

PEGGY.

Hush !

QUECKETT.

Let's settle one thing at a time. Who is Paulover ?

PEGGY.

Dear Dinah's husband.

QUECKETT.

Dear Dinah ?

PEGGY.

Your niece—Dinah Rankling.

QUECKETT.

Married ?

PEGGY.

Secretly. To Mr. Paulover.

[QUECKETT *puts his hand to his brow.*

QUECKETT.

Oh, that's old Paulover, is it ?

PEGGY.

Young Paulover. They were married really three weeks ago, but without any breakfast—I don't mean a bacon breakfast, I mean a proper breakfast. But we girls think they ought to have a wedding-cake and everything complete to start them in life together : and that's why you're giving this party, you know.

QUECKETT.

Now, understand me, I will not be dragged into such
a conspiracy !

PEGGY.

But you're in it.

QUECKETT.

The Ranklings are acquaintances of mine, almost
relatives; Admiral Rankling's cousin married the
sister of the man who bought my brother's horses.
[*Rubbing his hands together.*] I wash my hands of all
you vexing girls.

PEGGY.

Don't fret about it, please. Nothing can ever
make Mrs. Paulover Miss Rankling again. I'll go
and dress while you finish your letter.

QUECKETT.

[*Impatiently.*] Oh !

[*He resumes writing at the table.*

PEGGY.

[*Going to the door.*] The girls will be here directly.
Be nice, won't you ?

[*She goes out.* JANE *enters with tarts and
confectionery on dishes which she places
on the table before* QUECKETT.

JANE.

S'cuse me, sir.

[QUECKETT *rises with his letter and the
inkstand, and goes impatiently over to the
other side of the room, where he continues
writing on the top of piano.*

QUECKETT.

They won't let me write to the Insurance Office.

[TYLER *enters with some boxes of bon-bons.
The writing table being crowded,* JANE
waves him over to the piano and goes out.
TYLER *puts the bon-bons on the top of the
piano before* QUECKETT, *who snatches up
his letter and the inkstand again and
goes to the centre table.*

QUECKETT.

I *will* write to the Insurance Office.

[TYLER *goes out as* JANE *re-enters.*

JANE.

[*Presenting a bill.*] The pastrycook's bill, sir.

QUECKETT.

Great Scot! [*Diving his hand into his pocket,
bringing out some loose money and giving it to* JANE.]
There! [JANE *goes out.*] I've written to the Insurance
Office. [*Sealing the letter.*] My mind's easy—done my
duty to poor Caroline.

[*He puts the letter in his breast-pocket as*
TYLER *enters.*

TYLER.

[*More astonished than ever, announcing.*] Miss
Gwendoline Hawkins.

[GWENDOLINE *enters, dressed in a simple and
pretty party-dress.* TYLER *goes out.*

GWENDOLINE.

[*Bashfully, seeing nobody but* QUECKETT.] Oh, I'm first ; I shall come back again. [*She is going.*

QUECKETT.

Come in—come in. How d'ye do. [GWENDOLINE *advances.* QUECKETT *shakes hands with her.*] Delighted to see you—so glad you've come—won't you sit down ? [*To himself with satisfaction.*] Illustrations of Deportment and the Restrictions of Society—Vere Queckett. Carrie would be delighted.

TYLER *re-enters, still more astonished.*

TYLER.

Miss Hermyntrude Johnson, and—and—and Mrs. Reginald Paulover !

QUECKETT.

This is a little too vexing ! [ERMYNTRUDE *and* DINAH *enter, both prettily dressed—*DINAH *in white.* TYLER *goes out.* *Angrily.*] How d'ye do—so glad you've come—won't you sit down ?

DINAH.

We're very well, thank you.

ERMYNTRUDE.

Awfully well.

> [*They sit, the three girls in a row.* DINAH *in the centre,* GWENDOLINE *and* ERMYNTRUDE *taking her hands.*

QUECKETT.

[*To himself.*] Instructions in Polite Conversation.
[*Brusquely to* DINAH.] How is Paulover?

DINAH.

I think he's very well, thank you.

QUECKETT.

[*To himself.*] Carrie would be pleased. [*To the girls.*]
H'm! I suppose you young ladies distinctly understand that I occupy a painfully false position this
evening?

DINAH.

I am sure it is very, very kind of you to give this
party.

QUECKETT.

[*To himself.*] Well, now, that's exceedingly appropriate, the way in which that is put. Carrie really
does do her duty to the parents of these girls.

GWENDOLINE.

Peggy says you insist on our calling you Uncle.

QUECKETT.

Does she! [*To himself.*] Peggy is the one I've
turned against.

ERMYNTRUDE.

We think you'll be an awfully jolly uncle.

QUECKETT.

[*Pleased.*] Thank ye—thank ye. [*To himself.*] I

begin to like helping Carrie with the pupils. [PEGGY
*enters.   She is quaintly but untidily dressed in poor,
much-worn, and old fashioned finery.   In her hand she
carries a pair of soiled, long white gloves.*] Hallo!
[*Without speaking a word,* PEGGY *hurries across the
room and goes out.*] What is the matter with that
vexing girl now ? [PEGGY *re-enters with* TYLER, *push-
ing him forward.*]

TYLER.

[*Announcing.*] Miss Margaret Hesslerigge.

PEGGY *advances to* QUECKETT, *holding out her hand.*

PEGGY.

How do you do ?

QUECKETT.

[*Savagely.*] How d'ye do—delighted to see you—
for goodness' sake, sit down !

> [*He turns away to the fire.   The three girls
> rise to greet* PEGGY.

DINAH.

[*Anxiously.*] I don't think it's nearly half-past nine
yet.

PEGGY.

[*Rather proudly, produces a huge old-fashioned
watch.*] Twenty to ten.

DINAH.

I thought it was.

> [DINAH, GWENDOLINE, *and* ERMYNTRUDE *run
> to one window, pull aside the blind, and
> look out.* PEGGY *goes to the other win-

dow, pulls up the blind, and opens the window.

QUECKETT.

What are you doing?

PEGGY.

I can just see him, under his lamp post.

DINAH.

The fog will hurt him.

PEGGY.

Hush! I told him we'd whistle twice.

DINAH.

Do it!

[PEGGY *makes two or three ineffectual attempts to whistle.*

PEGGY.

Girls, it's ominous—my whistle has left me. [*To* QUECKETT, *taking his arm.*] Come and whistle!

QUECKETT.

No—no.

PEGGY.

[*Leading* QUECKETT *to the open window.*] Whistle, or you'll catch cold. [QUECKETT *whistles twice, desperately, then returns to the fireplace, annoyed.*] He's heard it. [*She closes the window and pulls down the blind.*] Now, listen. [*To* GWENDOLINE *and* ERMYNTRUDE.] You two girls count five.

GWENDOLINE.

One.

ERMYNTRUDE.

Two.

DINAH.

Oh, how slowly you count !

GWENDOLINE.

Three.

ERMYNTRUDE.

Four.

DINAH.

[*Clasping her hands.*] Five !

> [*There is a distant ring at the bell; with a little cry* DINAH *runs out.* PEGGY *begins to put her gloves on.* ERMYNTRUDE *and* GWENDOLINE *go to the door, open it and listen.*

PEGGY.

[*To* QUECKETT.] Thank you for whistling. I shall never make a " Whistling woman," shall I ?

QUECKETT.

A wide knowledge of humanity, in its highest and lowest grades, Miss Hesslerigge, does not enable me even to conjecture the possibilities of your future.

PEGGY.

No compliments, please. Thank you. [*She holds out her gloved hand for him to button the glove. After*

a look of astonishment he complies.] You know my
idea about my future, don't you?

QUECKETT.

No.

PEGGY.

That `I` only need one essential to become a
Duchess.

QUECKETT.

What is that?

PEGGY.

A Duke.

GWENDOLINE.

They're coming upstairs!

PEGGY.

[*To* QUECKETT.] Now you'll see Mr Paulover. Oh,
I do hope he'll take to you!

QUECKETT.

Well, really, I'm——

> [*He walks angrily away as* DINAH *enters
> with* REGINALD PAULOVER, *a good-
> looking lad, rather sheepish when in
> repose, but fiery and demonstrative when
> out of temper. He is in evening dress,
> overcoat, and muffler, and wears a res-
> pirator, which he removes on entering.*

DINAH.

[*Introducing the three girls.*] Reggie, these are my
three dear friends—Miss Hawkins—Miss Johnson——

E

REGINALD.

[*Bowing.*] Awfully pleased to meet you.

DINAH.

And Miss Hesslerigge.

> [PEGGY *advances and shakes hands with*
> REGINALD.

REGINALD.

Thank you very much for being so kind to—my wife.

ERMYNTRUDE.

[*To* GWENDOLINE, *disappointed.*] No whiskers or moustache! Oh !

PEGGY.

[*To* REGINALD.] Had you been waiting long ?

REGINALD.

Ten minutes. I was jolly glad to hear my wife's dear little whistle. I should know it from a thousand.

PEGGY.

H'm ! Dinah dear, make Mr. Paulover and Mr. Queckett known to each other.

> [QUECKETT *comes forward with a disagreeable
> look*. REGINALD *glares at him*.

DINAH.

[*Timidly.*] Reggie dear, this is Mr. Queckett.

> [QUECKETT *bows stiffly*. REGINALD *nods
> angrily*.

REGINALD.

[*To* DINAH.] Dinah, what is a man doing here?
You know I can't bear you to talk to a man.

DINAH.

Oh, Reggie, why are you always so jealous?

PEGGY.

Mr. Queckett is giving the party.

REGINALD

What party?

PEGGY.

Your wedding party.

REGINALD.

Is he! [*To* QUECKETT, *angrily.*] I'm much obliged
to Mr. Queckett.

PEGGY.

[*Pacifying* REGINALD.] Mr. Queckett is so nice—
he calls himself Dinah's uncle.

REGINALD.

Does he! Then it's a liberty—that's all I can
say.

QUECKETT.

Do you know you're in my house, sir?

REGINALD.

I'm not in your house, sir! Come away,
Dinah!

PEGGY.

Hush ! Mr. Queckett is Miss Dyott's——

QUECKETT.

Be quiet—mind your own business.

REGINALD.

[*To* QUECKETT.] At any rate it's my business, sir.

QUECKETT.

I'm afraid you're a cub, sir.

REGINALD.

What !

DINAH.

Oh, Reggie, don't !

[*A loud knock and ring are heard.*

PEGGY.

[*To* QUECKETT.]   Your friend.

REGINALD.

Whose friend ?

QUECKETT.

My friend.

REGINALD.

Another man, I suppose—Dinah !

PEGGY.

Ladies, do explain everything to Mr. Paulover.

[DINAH *seizes* REGINALD'S *arm.* GWENDOLINE
       and ERMYNTRUDE *gather round them,*
       REGINALD *protesting.*

REGINALD.

[*Handing his card as he passes* QUECKETT.] My card, sir.

QUECKETT.

Pooh, sir! [*Throwing the card in the fire. The three girls hurry* REGINALD *out of the room.*]

PEGGY.

[*To* QUECKETT.] I'm so sorry—he *hasn't* taken to you.

QUECKETT.

He needn't trouble himself! Upon my soul, this is going to be a nice party!

TYLER *enters.*

TYLER.

Three gentlemen, sir: I was to say the name of Mallory.

QUECKETT.

Three gentlemen!

PEGGY.

[*Delighted, to* QUECKETT.] Oh, he's brought some good fellows! [*Reckoning on her fingers.*] That's one for Ermyntrude—and one for me—and one for——

QUECKETT.

[*To* PEGGY.] Be quiet. [*To* TYLER.] I'll come down.

MALLORY.

[*Outside.*] Queckett!

QUECKETT.

Yes, Jack!

[*Jack Mallory enters. He is a good-look-
ing, jovial fellow of about thirty-six, with
a bronzed face. He is in evening dress
and overcoat.* Tyler *goes out.*

Mallory.

[*Shaking hands heartily with* Queckett.] Ah,
Queckett—dear old chap—well, I am glad to see
you.

Queckett.

How are you, Jack?

Mallory.

Quaint diggings you have up here. The hanging
committee have skied you, though, haven't they?
[*Seeing* Peggy.] I beg your pardon.

Queckett.

[*Confused.*] Oh—ah—yes. I didn't mention it.
I have my—my—nieces spending Christmas with
me.

Mallory.

[*Bowing to* Peggy.] Delighted. [*To* Queckett.]
Did you say niece or nieces?

Queckett.

Nieces. [*Softly to* Peggy, *quickly.*] How many?
I forget.

Peggy.

[*To* Queckett.] Three.

QUECKETT.

Three.

PEGGY.

Three, not counting me.

QUECKETT.

Three, not counting me. I mean three, not counting that vexing girl—Peggy—Margaret.

MALLORY.

[*Bowing.*] It would be impossible not to count Miss —Margaret.

PEGGY.

[*Simpering.*] Oh!

> [QUECKETT *assists* MALLORY *to take off his overcoat, first darting an angry look at* PEGGY.

PEGGY.

[*To herself.*] I shall give Gwendoline and Ermyntrude the two that are downstairs.

QUECKETT.

H'm! You're not alone, are you, Jack?

MALLORY.

No—they're coming up.

QUECKETT.

[*Grimly.*] Are they?

MALLORY.

The old gentleman takes his time with the stairs.

QUECKETT.

[*With forced ease.*] Poor old gentleman !   Who the deuce—— !

MALLORY.

The fact is, there's been a big Navy dinner to-night at the Whitehall Rooms.   The enthusiasm became rather forced—" Britannia rules the waves," and all that sort of thing—so I gladly thought of finishing up with you.   I've brought my nephew—hallo, here he is ! [MR SAUNDERS *enters.   He is a pretty boy, almost a child, in the uniform of a naval cadet.*]   My nephew—Horatio Nelson Drake Saunders, of the Training Ship " Dexterous."

SAUNDERS.

[*With the airs of a little man, but in a treble voice.*] How do you do ?   Awfully pleased to come here.

QUECKETT.

Glad to see you, Mr. Saunders.

MALLORY.

[*Laughing, to* SAUNDERS.] I say, you shouldn't have left the old gentleman.

SAUNDERS.

[*Laughing.*] He sent me up to count how many more stairs there were.

QUECKETT.

[*Impatiently.*] Jack, I don't put the question on theological grounds, but who *is* the old gentleman ?

MALLORY.

Oh, I beg your pardon—and his. We persuaded an old acquaintance of yours to join us—Admiral Rankling.

QUECKETT.

[*Aghast.*] What !

MALLORY.

Do you mind ?

QUECKETT.

Mind !

RANKLING.

[*Outside.*] Mr. Saunders !

SAUNDERS.

Here, sir.

> [PEGGY *makes a bolt out of the room.* SAUN-DERS *goes to the door, and returns with* RANKLING. RANKLING *is in evening dress, overcoat, and muffler, and is much out of breath.*

RANKLING.

Ah, Mr. Queckett, how do you do ? We haven't met anywhere lately ; I've been away, you know.

QUECKETT.

I am delighted to renew our acquaintance, Admiral Rankling.

RANKLING.

[*Puffing.*] Mr. Mallory suggested that we should smoke our last cigar at your lodgings. I can't stay, for I've a long distance to drive home. At least, I suppose I have, for I really don't know quite where we are. What quarter of London have you brought me to, Mr. Mallory? Oh, thank ye!

> [*He turns to* SAUNDERS, *who is offering to remove his overcoat. The door is slightly opened, and the heads of all the girls are seen.*

QUECKETT.

[*Hastily to* MALLORY.] He doesn't know where he is!

MALLORY.

The fog's as thick as a board outside.

QUECKETT.

He isn't aware he lives a hundred and fifty yards off!

MALLORY.

No—does he?

QUECKETT.

Hush, don't tell him! Jack, don't tell him! I'll explain why by and bye.

> [QUECKETT *turns to assist* SAUNDERS *who, mounted on a chair, is struggling ineffectually to relieve* RANKLING *of his overcoat.*

RANKLING.

Thank ye—bits o' boys, bits o' boys.

MALLORY.

[*To himself.*] There's a wild look about poor Queckett I don't like. It's his lonely bachelor life, I suppose. Curious place too—he used to be such a swell in the Albany. [*Looking about him. The door shuts and the heads disappear.*]

RANKLING.

[*To* QUECKETT.] Thank ye—thank ye [*Panting.*] Ouf!

> [RANKLING *sits down, and* MALLORY *talks to him.* SAUNDERS *has seated himself on the sofa and is dozing off, quite tired out.*

QUECKETT.

Oh, what a party!

> [*The door opens, and* PEGGY's *head appears.*

PEGGY.

[*Hurriedly to* QUECKETT.] Who'd have thought of this?

QUECKETT.

It might be worse—he doesn't recognise the house he is in.

PEGGY.

Doesn't he?

QUECKETT.

Get rid of his daughter and that horrid Paulover.

PEGGY.

Certainly not; I know he won't recognise his daughter.

QUECKETT.

Won't recognise his own dau—— You'll drive me
mad !

> [*They continue to talk in undertones.* SAUN-
> DERS *is now fast asleep.*

RANKLING.

[*To* MALLORY.] No—*I* don't like the look of poor
Queckett.

MALLORY.

He seems altered.

RANKLING.

Altered—he glares like the devil.   He's not
married, is he ?

MALLORY.

No.

RANKLING.

Then, what does he mean by it ?   Queer rooms
too.   [*Catching sight of the wedding-cake on the table.*]
Lord, look there !

MALLORY.

[*Looking at the cake.*] Hallo !

RANKLING.

Why, it's like the thing we had at my wedding
breakfast.   Phew !   I shall go.

MALLORY.

No, no !   The fact is poor old Queckett has some
nieces staying with him.

RANKLING.

Nieces?

MALLORY.

Four of 'em. I've seen one, and I fancy by the look of her mischievous little face, that they're too much for him.

PEGGY.

[*To* QUECKETT.] Leave everything to me. Don't spoil the party, uncle.

QUECKETT.

Dash the party!

> [PEGGY *retiring hastily, the door bangs, at which* RANKLING *and* MALLORY *look round.*

RANKLING.

Oh, Queckett, where are your nieces?

QUECKETT.

Nieces—nieces? Oh, they retire at eight o'clock. Early to bed, early to rise——

> [GWENDOLINE *and* ERMYNTRUDE *enter, visibly pushed on by* PEGGY.

RANKLING.

[*Rising.*] Um, this doesn't look like early to bed.

QUECKETT.

[*Weakly.*] Just got up, I suppose. Gwendoline— Ermyntrude—my dears—Admiral Rankling—Mr.

Mallory—[*Looking about for* SAUNDERS.] Mr.—Mr.—
Oh, Mr. Saunders is asleep !

[ERMYNTRUDE *and* GWENDOLINE *advance to*
RANKLING.

RANKLING.

[*To the girls.*] How do you do ?　And whose
daughters are you ?

[GWENDOLINE *and* ERMYNTRUDE *look frightened, and shake their heads.*

QUECKETT.

Oh, these are my sister Isabel's girls.

RANKLING.

Why, all your sister Isabel's children were boys.

QUECKETT.

Were boys, yes.

RANKLING.

[*Irritably.*] *Are* boys, sir.

QUECKETT.

Are *men*, now. H'm !　I should have said these
are my sister Janet's children.

RANKLING.

Oh !　I've never heard of your sister Janet.

QUECKETT.

No—quiet, retiring girl, Janet.

RANKLING.

Well, then, whom did Janet marry?

QUECKETT.

Whom *didn't* Janet marry! I mean, whom *did* Janet marry? Why, Finch Griffin of the Berkshire Royals!

RANKLING.

Dear me, we're going to meet Major Griffin and his wife on Christmas Day at the Trotwells'.

QUECKETT.

Are you? [*To* GWENDOLINE *and* ERMYNTRUDE.] Go away. [PEGGY *enters.*] Oh—ahem! This is Margaret —Peggy.

RANKLING.

Oh—another of Mrs. Griffin's.

QUECKETT.

Yes, yes!

RANKLING.

Large family.

QUECKETT.

Rapid—two a year.

RANKLING.

[*Eyeing* PEGGY.] Why, we've met before to-day!

QUECKETT.

Eh—where?

RANKLING.

At a miserable school near my house in Portland Place.

PEGGY.

Oh, yes. Our holidays began this afternoon.

RANKLING.

Why, Queckett, my daughter Dinah and Miss Griffin are school-fellows!

QUECKETT.

No!

RANKLING.

Yes!

QUECKETT.

No!

RANKLING.

Yes, sir.

QUECKETT.

How small the world is!

RANKLING.

Do you happen to know anything about the person who keeps that school? What's the woman's name —Miss—Miss—— ?

QUECKETT.

Miss—Miss—Miss——

PEGGY.

Miss Dyott. Oh, yes, Uncle knows her to speak to.

RANKLING.

What about her, Queckett?

QUECKETT.

[*Looking vindictively at* PEGGY.] Er—um—rather not hazard an opinion.

[*He hastily joins* MALLORY, GWENDOLINE, *and* ERMYNTRUDE.

RANKLING.

[*Confidentially to* PEGGY.] Er—um—my dear Miss Griffin, did you receive a short but ample apology from me this afternoon—addressed, " To the young lady who was shaken " ?

PEGGY.

Yes; and oh! I shall always prize it !

RANKLING.

No, no, don't ! You haven't bothered your Uncle about it, have you, dear ?

PEGGY.

No—not yet.

RANKLING.

I shouldn't, then ; I shouldn't. He seems worried enough. Shall I take you and your sisters to see the pantomime ?

PEGGY.

Yes—please.

RANKLING.

Then you'd better give me back that apology.

PEGGY.

Oh, no—you'd use it again.

RANKLING.

One—two—three. Mr. Mallory says you have *four* nieces with you, Mr. Queckett.

QUECKETT.

Ah, but Jack's been dining, you know. I beg your pardon, Jack.

PEGGY.

Oh, yes, there is one more. Mrs.—Mrs.—Parkinson is here with her husband.

QUECKETT.

H'm! my brother Tankerville's eldest girl.

RANKLING.

I've never heard of your brother Tankerville!

QUECKETT.

No—he's Deputy Inspector of Prisons in British Guiana. Quiet, retiring chap.

PEGGY.

I'll go and fetch them. [*She runs out.*

QUECKETT.

[*To* RANKLING.] To make a clean breast of it, the girls have been preparing a little festival to-night in honour of Mr. and Mrs.—Mr. and Mrs.— the name Peggy mentioned. My niece was married, very quietly, some weeks ago to a charming young fellow — a charming young fellow—and these foolish children insist on cutting a wedding-cake and all that sort of nonsense. I didn't want to disturb you with their chatter——

RANKLING.

You forget, Queckett, you are speaking to a father.

QUECKETT.

No—I don't, indeed.

PEGGY *re-enters, followed by* REGINALD *and* DINAH.

PEGGY.

My cousin and Mr. Parkinson.

RANKLING.

How do you—— [*Staring.*] What an extraordinary likeness to my brother Ned! [*Taking her hand slowly, still looking at her.*] And how do you do?

DINAH.

[*Palpitating.*] Thank you, I am very well.

RANKLING.

Do you know, your voice is exceedingly like my sister Rachel's!

REGINALD.

[*Thrusting himself between* DINAH *and* RANKLING.] I am sorry to differ—I think my wife resembles no one but herself.

RANKLING.

[*Hotly.*] I beg your pardon, sir.

REGINALD.

[*Hotly.*] Pray, don't!

RANKLING.

[*To himself.*]   *That's* not   a   charming   young
fellow !

PEGGY.

[*Presenting* MALLORY *to* DINAH.] Mr. Mallory.

MALLORY.

[*Gallantly, to* DINAH.] I am delighted to have the
opportunity of congratulating my old friend's niece
upon her recent marriage.   [*Taking her hand.*] I
think myself especially fortunate in being present on
such——

REGINALD.

[*Thrusting himself between* DINAH *and* MALLORY,
and giving DINAH *his arm.*] How do you do, sir ?

PEGGY.

Mr. Mallory—Mr. Parkinson.

[*They bow abruptly, glaring at each other.*

MALLORY.

[*To himself.*] Is *that* a charming young fellow ?

> [DINAH *expostulates in undertones with*
> REGINALD; *he answering with violent*
> *gestures and glaring at* RANKLING, *who*
> *mutters comments on* DINAH'S *resem-*
> *blance to various members of his family.*

*PEGGY endeavours to pacify MALLORY
who is evidently annoyed, and altogether
there is much hubbub, with signs of general
ill-feeling.*

QUECKETT.

[*Sinking back in his chair.*] Oh, what a party!

JANE *enters.*

JANE.

[*Quietly to QUECKETT.*] The pudding is in the arey, sir, waiting to be paid.

QUECKETT.

I'll come to it. [*JANE goes out. To PEGGY.*] Margaret, show Admiral Rankling and Mr. Mallory where the cigarettes are—they may like—— [*To himself.*] Years are going off my life! [*He goes out.*

PEGGY.

[*To MALLORY.*] May I take you to the cigarettes?

MALLORY.

[*To PEGGY.*] You may take me anywhere.

PEGGY.

[*Bashfully.*] Oh! [*To RANKLING.*] The cigarettes are in the next room, Admiral Rankling.

RANKLING.

[*Not hearing PEGGY, but still eyeing DINAH.*] That girl has a look of Emma's sister Susan.

[*Peggy and* Mallory *go out.* Reginald
seeing Rankling *is still looking at* Dinah,
*abruptly takes her over to the door, glaring
at* Rankling *as he passes.*

Reginald.

[*To* Dinah, *fiercely.*] Come away, Dinah!

Dinah.

[*To* Reginald, *tearfully.*] Oh, Reggie, dear Reggie,
you are so different when people are not present.

[*They go out.* Rankling *watches them through
the doorway.* Gwendoline *has meanwhile
seated herself beside* Saunders, *whose head
has gradually fallen till it rests upon
her shoulder. She is now sitting quite
still, looking down upon the boy's face.*

Ermyntrude.

[*Watching them enviously.*] Well, considering that
Mr. Saunders was introduced to us asleep, I don't
think Gwendoline's behaviour is *comme il faut!* [*She
bumps gently against* Rankling.] Oh!

Rankling.

[*Looking at* Ermyntrude, *rather dazed.*] My dear, I
am quite glad to see somebody who isn't like any of
my relations. Come along.

[*They go out.* Saunders *moves dreamily
and murmurs.*]

SAUNDERS.

[*Waking.*] All right, ma dear, I'll come down directly. [*He raises his head and kisses* GWENDOLINE, *then opens his eyes and looks at her, startled.*] Oh, I've been dreaming about my ma! I—I don't know you, do I?

GWENDOLINE.

It doesn't matter, Mr. Saunders. You've had such a good sleep. [*She kisses his forehead gently.*

SAUNDERS.

Oh, that's just like my ma! Where are the others?

GWENDOLINE.

[*Arranging his curls upon his forehead.*] I'll take you to them.

SAUNDERS.

Thank you. What's your name?

GWENDOLINE.

Gwendoline.

SAUNDERS.

Gwen's short for that, isn't it? [*Rubbing his eyes with his fists, then offering her his arm.*] Permit me, Gwen.

> [*They go out.* QUECKETT, *his hair disarranged, his appearance generally wild, immediately enters, followed by* JANE *and* TYLER.

QUECKETT.

I can't help it! I am in the hands of fate. Arrange the table. I cannot help it!

[TYLER *and* JANE *proceed to arrange the table
and the seats for supper.* PEGGY *enters
quietly.*

PEGGY.

It is supper-time.   Oh, what's the matter, Uncle
Vere?

QUECKETT.

Well, in the first place, there are no oysters.

PEGGY.

I've seen them!

QUECKETT.

I've gone further—I've tasted them.

PEGGY.

Bad!

QUECKETT.

Well, I should describe them as Inland oysters.   A
long time since *they* had a fortnight at the sea-
side.

PEGGY.

Oh, dear!   Then we must fall back on the lark
pudding.

QUECKETT.

You'll injure yourself seriously if you do.

PEGGY.

Tell me everything.   It has not come small?

QUECKETT.

It has come ridiculously small.

PEGGY.

It was ordered for eight persons.

QUECKETT.

Then it is architecturally disproportionate.

PEGGY.

[*To herself.*] Something must be done. [*She runs to the writing-table and begins to write rapidly on three half-sheets of paper, folding each into a three-cornered note as she finishes it.*] The girls must be warned. [*Writing.*] " For goodness' sake, don't taste the pudding." Poor girls—what an end to a happy day !

QUECKETT.

[*To himself.*] Oh, if the members of my family could see me at this moment ! I, whose suppers in the Albany were at one time a proverb ! Oh, Caroline, Caroline, even you little know the sacrifice I have made for you !

PEGGY.

[*To* QUECKETT, *handing him the notes.*] Quick, please quick—give them these notes.

QUECKETT.

[*Taking the notes.*] What for ?

PEGGY.

Oh, don't ask ; you will see the result.

QUECKETT.

But you mustn't write to people you—— !

PEGGY.

[*Angrily.*] Go away!

[*He hurries out.* PEGGY *wipes her eyes.*

JANE.

Oh, don't be upset, Miss!

PEGGY.

No, I won't, I won't. But I am only a girl, and the responsibility is very great for such young shoulders.

> [*There is a murmur of voices outside.* JANE *and* TYLER *go out as* RANKLING *enters with* ERMYNTRUDE, *followed by* REGGIE *with* DINAH. REGINALD *is endeavouring to keep her away from* MALLORY, *who comes after them.* SAUNDERS *and* GWENDOLINE *follow next, and* QUECKETT *brings up the rear. There is much talking as* QUECKETT *indicates the seats they are to occupy.*

PEGGY.

[*Quietly to* QUECKETT.] Did you give the girls the notes?

QUECKETT.

[*Surprised.*] No.

PEGGY.

Oh! Never mind—I'll whisper to them now.

> [*She whispers hurriedly to* DINAH, GWENDO-LINE, *and* ERMYNTRUDE.

QUECKETT.

[*To himself.*] I didn't understand they were for the girls.

> [*He goes to the head of the table as* RANKLING,
> MALLORY, *and* SAUNDERS *come suddenly
> together, each carrying a note.*

RANKLING.

[*To* MALLORY.] Mallory, we were right—there is some horrible mystery about Queckett. [*Looking to see they are not observed.*] I've had an anonymous warning. " For heaven's sake, don't touch the pudding! "

MALLORY.

I know.

RANKLING.

Tell the boy.

MALLORY.

[*To* SAUNDERS.] I say—don't you say yes to pudding.

SAUNDERS.

I know. Tell the old gentleman.

MALLORY.

[*To* SAUNDERS.] He knows. [*To* RANKLING.] He knows.

> [*With a simultaneous gesture they pocket the
> notes and go to find their seats at table.
> They all sit. The lobster salad and the
> pâté have been placed by* TYLER *at the end
> of the table.* TYLER *now enters carrying
> nine large plates, which he places before*
> QUECKETT.

QUECKETT.

[*With assumed composure and good spirits.*] There
is a spontaneity about our jolly little supper which
will perhaps—ah'm!—atone for any absence of elabor-
ation.

RANKLING.

Don't name it, Mr. Queckett.

MALLORY.

Just as it should be, my dear fellow.

[TYLER *goes out.*

QUECKETT.

The language of the heart is simplicity.   Our little
supper is from the heart.

MALLORY.

Ah, I shall never forget your little suppers in the
Albany—where were they from?

QUECKETT.

Gunters', Jack.   [*With a groan.*] Oh!

[JANE, *at the door, hands to* TYLER *a very
small pudding in a silver basin, which he
places before* QUECKETT.

RANKLING, MALLORY, *and* SAUNDERS.

[*To themselves.*] The pudding!

[*They exhibit great eagerness to get a view of
the pudding.*

PEGGY.

[*Behind* MALLORY'S *back.*] Oh, how shameful it looks !

QUECKETT.

[*Falteringly.*] Here is a homely little dish which has fascinations for many, though I never touch it myself—I never touch it myself. [RANKLING, MALLORY, *and* SAUNDERS *exchange significant looks.*] Ah'm ! A pudding made of larks. [*He glances round, all look down, there is deep silence.*] A pudding—made—of larks. [*To* DINAH.] My dear—a very little ?

DINAH.

No, thank you, Uncle.

QUECKETT.

Perhaps you're right. Gwendoline, a suggestion ?

GWENDOLINE.

No, thank you, Uncle.

QUECKETT.

[*To* PEGGY.] Margaret, I know what your digestion is—I won't tempt you. [*To* ERMYNTRUDE.] Ermyntrude—the least in the world ?

ERMYNTRUDE.

No, thank you, Uncle.

QUECKETT.

[*To himself.*] Ah ! How lucky !

PEGGY.

[*To herself.*] Bravo girls; I was afraid they'd falter.

QUECKETT.

[*Heartily.*] Now then—Admiral Rankling?

RANKLING.

No, thank you.

QUECKETT.

No pudding?

RANKLING.

I haven't long dined, thank you, Queckett.

QUECKETT.

[*To* REGINALD—*coldly.*] May I?

REGINALD.

[*Distantly.*] I never eat suppers, thank you.

QUECKETT.

[*To* SAUNDERS.] My dear Mr. Saunders?

SAUNDERS.

No, Mr. Queckett, thank you.

QUECKETT.

[*Getting desperate—to* MALLORY.] Jack—a lark?

MALLORY.

No, thanks, old fellow.

QUECKETT.

Well, I—— [*Throwing down his knife and spoon, and leaning back in his chair. To* TYLER.] Take it away!

> [TYLER *removes the pudding; they all watch its going.*

TYLER.

[*Handing it to* JANE.] Keep it warm, Jane.

QUECKETT.

Jack, a lobster salad and a small *pâté de foie gras* are at your end of the table.

MALLORY.

[*Looking round.*] May I?

> [*There is a general reply of* "No, thank you," *expressed in symbols by the ladies.*

PEGGY.

[*To herself.*] Poor girls, what sacrifices they make for these men!

MALLORY.

[*With a plate in his hand.*] May I—— ?

RANKLING, SAUNDERS, *and* REGINALD.

[*Together.*] No, thank you.

QUECKETT.

[*To himself.*] What a supper party! Tyler, the champagne.

[T YLER *fetches a bottle of champayne, and proceeds to open it.*

RANKLING.

[*Behind* ERMYNTRUDE *and* PEGGY, *to* MALLORY.] If we see the cork drawn, shall we risk it?

MALLORY.

[*To* RANKLING.] Risk it.

RANKLING.

Risk it.

[REGINALD *has risen from the table and is seen tapping* SAUNDERS *upon the shoulder and speaking to him rapidly and excitedly.*

SAUNDERS.

No, I have not!

[*Talking together,* REGINALD *and* SAUNDERS *go out hurriedly.*

MALLORY.

What's the matter with that charming young fellow now? [*To the table.*] Excuse me.

[*He follows them out.*

DINAH.

[*Tearfully to* GWENDOLINE.] Reginald's jealousy gets worse and worse. I am sure it will cloud our future.

GWENDOLINE.

[*To* DINAH.] Mr. Saunders wasn't looking at you, I am positive. The poor little fellow was stroking my hand.

[MALLORY *returns with* SAUNDERS *and* REGINALD, *who both look excited, and their hair is disarranged.*

REGINALD.

[*To* MALLORY *and* SAUNDERS.] I beg your pardon; I may have been mistaken. I imagined that Mr. Saunders was regarding my wife in a way which overstepped the borders of ordinary admiration.

[*They hastily shake hands all round and hurry back to their seats.* TYLER *has poured out the champagne, and now departs.* ADMIRAL RANKLING *rises.* QUECKETT *taps the table for silence.*

QUECKETT.

Please—please.

RANKLING.

Ah'm !

MALLORY.

[*To himself.*] I thought the old gentleman wouldn't resist the temptation.

RANKLING.

My dear Mr. Queckett, it would ill become an old man—himself the father of a daughter, nearly, if not quite, of the age of the young lady opposite me—to lose an opportunity of saying a few words on the

G

pleasant, the—the extremely pleasant—condition of the British Naval Forces—ah'm! no——

MALLORY.

[*To himself.*] I knew that would happen.

RANKLING.

Pardon me, I have been speaking on other subjects to-night. I should say, the extremely pleasant occasion which brings us together.

QUECKETT.

Certainly, my dear Rankling, how nice of you!

RANKLING.

Not only am I the commander—the father—of a ship—of a daughter whom it is my ambition to see happily wedded to the man of her choice——

PEGGY.

Hear, hear!

QUECKETT.

[*In an undertone, glaring at her.*] You vexing girl.

RANKLING.

But I am also the husband of a heavily-plated cruiser—er—um—h'm! of a dear lady to whose affection and society I owe the greatest happiness of my life.

PEGGY.

[*To herself.*] How different some gentlemen are when their wives are not present.

RANKLING.

If I have the regret of knowing that my acquaintance with Mrs.—Mrs.——

PEGGY.

Parkinson.

RANKLING.

Thank you, I know—Parkinson—has begun only to-night, I have also the pleasure of inaugurating a friendship with that delightful young lady, which on my side shall be little less than paternal. I—I—I——

MALLORY.

Oh, gracious!

RANKLING.

I—I cannot sit down——

MALLORY.

[*Wearily.*] Why not!

RANKLING.

I will not sit down without adding a word of congratulation to Mr.—Mr.——

PEGGY.

Parkinson.

RANKLING.

Thank you, I know—Parkinson—the young gentleman whose ingenious construction and sea-going qualities——

MALLORY.

No—no.

RANKLING.

Er—um—whose amiability and genial demeanour
have so favourably impressed us.   As an old married
man I welcome this recruit to the service.

PEGGY.

Hear, hear !

RANKLING.

It is one of hardship and danger—of stiff breezes
and dismal night watches.   But it is because Englishmen never know when they are beaten——

MALLORY.

No, no.

RANKLING.

Yes, sir—it is because Englishmen never know
when they are beaten that they occasionally find
conjugal happiness.   I ask you all to drink to the
Navy—to—to Mr. and Mrs.—thank you, I know—
Jenkinson.

> [*All except* DINAH *and* REGINALD *rise and*
> *drink the toast* "Mr. and Mrs. Parkinson,"
> *then, as they resume their seats,* REGINALD
> *rises sulkily.*

REGINALD.

Admiral Rankling.

> [JANE *appears at the door, wildly beckoning*
> *to* QUECKETT.

JANE.

[*In a whisper.*] Sir—Sir——— !

QUECKETT.

[*Angrily.*] Not now—not now—go away.

THE GIRLS.

Hush !.
        [*The* GIRLS *motion* JANE *away; she retires.*

QUECKETT.

[*To* REGINALD.] I beg pardon.

REGINALD.

All I have to say is that the highest estimation
Admiral Rankling can form of me will not do justice
to my devotion to my wife.

PEGGY.

[*Sotto voce.*] Oh, beautiful !

REGINALD.

[*Fiercely.*] And I should like to know the individual,
old or young, who would take my wife from me !

MALLORY.

[*To himself.*] Many a husband would like to know
that person.

REGINALD.

In conclusion—as for Admiral Rankling's offer of a
paternal friendship, I trust he will remember that
offer if ever we should have occasion to remind him of
it. [*Looking at his watch.*] And now I regret to
say——   [*The girls rise, the men follow.*

PEGGY.

No, no—not before we have danced one quadrille.

GWENDOLINE *and* ERMYNTRUDE.

Oh, yes—oh, yes!   A quadrille !

PEGGY.

Uncle Vere will play for us.

QUECKETT.

No, Uncle Vere will not !

MALLORY.

Oh, yes you will, Queckett, old fellow—eh ?

QUECKETT.

Well—I—with pleasure, Jack.   [*To himself.*] How dare they !

PEGGY.

Clear the floor !

> [SAUNDERS *and* MALLORY, *assisted by* ERMYN-
> TRUDE *and* GWENDOLINE, *put back the
> table and chairs.*

RANKLING.

[*Getting very good-humoured.*] Upon my soul, I never saw such girls in my life !   I wonder whether my Dinah is anything like 'em !

> [DINAH *and* REGINALD *are having a violent
> altercation.*

DINAH.

A wife shouldn't dance with her husband—it is horrible form!

REGINALD.

I can't see you led out by a stranger.

DINAH.

It is merely a quadrille.

REGINALD.

Merely a quadrille! Woman, do you think I am marble!

DINAH.

[*Distractedly, turning to* RANKLING.] Admiral Rankling, are you going to dance?

RANKLING.

[*Gallantly.*] If you do me the honour, my dear Madam. [*She takes his arm.*

REGINALD.

[*Madly, to* DINAH.] Ah, flirt!

QUECKETT.

[*To* PEGGY.] Get rid of them soon, or I shall become a gibbering idiot!

MALLORY.

[*Slapping* QUECKETT *on the back.*] Now then, Queckett. [QUECKETT *goes to the piano. To* PEGGY.] Will you make me happy, dear Miss Peggy?

PEGGY.

Thank you, Mr. Mallory, I never dance. [*Taking his arm.*] But I don't mind this once. Uncle!

QUECKETT.

[*To himself.*] I wash my hands of the entire party!

[*He plays the first figure of a quadrille, while they dance*—RANKLING *and* DINAH, SAUNDERS *and* GWENDOLINE, MALLORY *and* PEGGY, ERMYNTRUDE *and* REGINALD. *They dance with brightness and animation, but whenever* REGINALD *encounters* DINAH *there is a violent altercation. As the figure ends* JANE *enters again, and runs to* QUECKETT *at the piano.*

QUECKETT.

What is it?

JANE.

Oh, sir, do come down-stairs—as far down as you can get.

QUECKETT.

What do you mean?

JANE.

That boy, Tyler, sir!

QUECKETT.

Tyler—well?

JANE.

He went off bang in the kitchen, sir, about ten minutes ago. Them fireworks!

QUECKETT.

Fireworks! Where is he?

JANE.

Gone for the engines, sir.

QUECKETT.

[*Rising.*] The engines!

ERMYNTRUDE.

Uncle!

GWENDOLINE.

Uncle Vere!

PEGGY.

Now then, Uncle!

QUECKETT.

Excuse me—let somebody take my place at the piano.
I—I'll be back in a moment!

[JANE *hurries out, he following her.*

PEGGY.

[*Running to the piano and commencing a waltz.*] A
waltz! Change partners!

[RANKLING *dances with* ERMYNTRUDE, SAUN-
DERS *with* GWENDOLINE. REGINALD *is left
out, but is wildly following* DINAH, *who is
dancing with* MALLORY.

RANKLING.

[*Puffing.*] Not so fast, Miss Griffin—not so fast.

REGINALD.

[*In* DINAH's *ear.*] I shall require some explanation, Madam.

DINAH.

Oh, Reginald !

> [*There is the sound of a prolonged knocking at the street door, followed by a bell ringing violently.*

PEGGY.

[*Playing.*] Somebody wants to come in, evidently.

> [*Suddenly the music and the dancing stop and everybody listens ; then they all run to the windows and look out.*

RANKLING.

What's that ?

MALLORY.

What's wrong ?

SAUNDERS.

Oh, look there !

PEGGY.

Oh, there's such a crowd at our house ?

> [QUECKETT *re-enters with* JANE, *who sinks into a chair.* QUECKETT *looks very pale and frightened.*

QUECKETT.

Listen to me, please.

ALL.

What's the matter ?

QUECKETT.

Don't be alarmed. Look at me. Imitate my self-possession.

ALL.

What *is* the matter?

QUECKETT.

The matter? The weather is so unfavourable that the boy Tyler has been compelled to display fireworks on the premises.

THE GIRLS.

Oh!

THE MEN.

What has happened?

QUECKETT.

Pray don't be disturbed. There is not the slightest occasion for alarm. We have now the choice of one alternative.

RANKLING *and* MALLORY.

What's that?

QUECKETT.

To get out without unnecessary delay.

THE GIRLS.

[*Clustering together.*] Oh!

RANKLING.

[*Assuming the tone of a commander.*] Mr. Mallory! Mr. Saunders!

MALLORY.

Yes, sir.

SAUNDERS.

Yes, sir.

[MALLORY *and* SAUNDERS *place themselves beside* RANKLING.

RANKLING.

Ladies, fetch your cloaks and wraps preparatory to breaking up our pleasant little party. Who volunteers to assist the ladies?

MALLORY.

I, sir!

SAUNDERS.

I, sir!

REGINALD.

I do!

QUECKETT.

I do!

RANKLING.

Mr. Mallory, tell off Mr. Queckett and Mr. Jenkinson to help the ladies.

[*The girls run out, followed by* REGINALD, QUECKETT, *and* JANE.

RANKLING.

Mr. Mallory! Mr. Saunders!

MALLORY *and* SAUNDERS.

Yes, sir.

RANKLING.

Our respective coats.

[*They bustle about to get their coats as the door quietly opens and* JAFFRAY, *a fireman, appears.*

JAFFRAY.

Good evening, gentlemen. Can you tell me where I'll find the ladies?

MALLORY.

They're putting on their hats and cloaks.

JAFFRAY.

Thank you, gentlemen, I'm much obliged to you. [*He goes to the window, pulls up the blind, and throws the window open; the top of a ladder is seen against the balcony.*] Are you coming up, Mr. Goff?

GOFF.

[*Out of sight.*] Yes, Mr. Jaffray.

[GOFF, *a middle-aged, jolly-looking fireman, enters by the balcony and the window.*

JAFFRAY.

Gentlemen, Mr. Goff—one of the oldest and most respected members of the Brigade. Mr. Goff tells some most interesting stories, gentlemen.

RANKLING.

[*Impatiently*] Stories, sir! Call the ladies, Mr. Mallory. [MALLORY *goes out.*

GOFF.

I shouldn't hurry them, sir—ladies like to take

their time. Now I remember an instance in October '78——

RANKLING.

Confound it, sir, you're not going to relate anecdotes now!

JAFFRAY.

I beg your pardon, sir, Mr. Goff is one of the most experienced and entertaining members of the Brigade.

RANKLING.

I tell you I don't care about that just now! Where are the ladies?   [SAUNDERS *goes out.*

JAFFRAY.

Excuse me, sir, Mr. Goff's reminiscences are well worth hearing while you wait.

RANKLING.

But I don't wish to wait!

> [MALLORY *and* PEGGY, SAUNDERS *and* GWENDOLINE, REGINALD *and* DINAH, *followed by* JANE, *enter. The girls are hastily attired in all sorts of odd apparel and carrying bonnet-boxes, parcels, and small hand-bags.* ERMYNTRUDE *carries, amongst other things, a cage of white mice,* GWENDOLINE, *a bird in a cage, and* DINAH *a black cat, and* PEGGY *a pair of skates and a brush and comb.*

THE GIRLS.

We're ready.   Take us away!

JAFFRAY.

I must really ask you, ladies and gentlemen, to take it quietly for a few minutes.

ALL.

Take it quietly! What for?

JAFFRAY.

The staircase isn't just the thing for ladies and gentlemen at the present moment. I shall have to ask the ladies and gentlemen to use the Escape.

ALL.

[*Turning to the window.*] The Escape! Where is it?

JAFFRAY.

It'll be here in two minutes. In the meantime, I think Mr. Goff could wile away the time very pleasantly with a reminiscence or two. Ladies, Mr. Goff——

THE GIRLS.

Oh, take us away! Take us away!

> [MALLORY, SAUNDERS, *and* REGINALD *soothe the ladies*, JAFFRAY *goes to the window and looks out.*

GOFF.

[*Pleasantly seating himself and taking off his helmet.*] Well, ladies, I don't know that I can tell you much to amuse you—however——

RANKLING.

Be quiet, sir—we will not be entertained!

JAFFRAY.

[*Carrying a hose from the window to the door.*]
Really, gentlemen, I must say I've never heard Mr.
Goff treated so hasty at any conflagration.

[*He carries the hose out.*

RANKLING.

A fireman full of anecdote! I decline to appreciate any reminiscence whatever. So do we all!

REGINALD.

Certainly!

MALLORY.

All of us!

GOFF.

It was in July '79, ladies—my wife had just
brought my tea to the Chandos Street Station——

[JAFFRAY *re-enters, and goes to the window.*

MALLORY.

Will you be silent, sir?

REGINALD.

Get up and do something!

SAUNDERS.

Go away!

JAFFRAY.

The Escape, ladies and gentlemen—that window—
one at a time.

> [*There is a general movement and hubbub.
> GOFF rises, he and JAFFRAY disappear by
> the window on the left. MALLORY throws
> open the other window, and JAFFRAY
> appears outside and receives DINAH,
> GWENDOLINE, ERMYNTRUDE, PEGGY, and
> JANE as they escape.*

RANKLING.

Mr. Mallory—Mr. Saunders—good evening!

> [REGINALD *disappears by the right-hand
> window. SAUNDERS goes after him,
> MALLORY is about to follow when
> QUECKETT enters hurriedly. QUECKETT
> is in a tall hat, a short covert coat, and
> carries gloves and an umbrella. He is
> flourishing a letter.*

QUECKETT.

[*Pulling* MALLORY *back.*] Jack—Jack!

MALLORY.

Hallo!

QUECKETT.

I'm going back to save some valuables. Directly
you get down, post that letter. Oh, Jack, it's so
important.

MALLORY.

[*Looking at the letter.*] To the Eagle Fire Insurance Company.

QUECKETT.

Quite so—slipped my memory.

[MALLORY *disappears.* JAFFRAY *follows him.*

RANKLING.

[*Hurrying to* QUECKETT.] My dear Queckett, it is the commander's duty to be the last to leave the ship—you are master here. Thank you for your hospitality. Good-night.

QUECKETT.

My dear Rankling, thank *you* for coming to see me. Good-night.

JAFFRAY *appears at the window.*

JAFFRAY.

It's all right, gentlemen—there's a kind lady down below who is taking everybody into her house for the night—Mrs. Rankling of Portland Place.

RANKLING.

Mrs. Rankling—that's my wife !

[QUECKETT *disappears.*

JAFFRAY.

Is she, sir ? Glad to hear it. Then they are all your visitors till to-morrow.

RANKLING.

Confound it, sir, where do I live?

JAFFRAY.

Just at the corner here, sir—a hundred yards off.

RANKLING.

Then where am I now?

JAFFRAY.

Miss Dyott's boarding school, sir—Volumnia College.

RANKLING.

What!

[*He and* JAFFRAY *go out by the window on the right as* GOFF *enters by the window on the left.*

GOFF.

Where is he? [*Calling at the door.*] Sir, here's the lady of the house—rode up on an engine from Piccadilly—make haste—she says she will come up the ladder.

QUECKETT *enters quickly dragging after him several boxes of cigars.*

QUECKETT.

A lady! What lady? [MISS DYOTT *appears at the window. She is in the gorgeous dress of an opera-*

*bouffe Queen, with a flaxen wig, much disarranged, and
a crown on one side.   Recoiling.*] Caroline!

MISS DYOTT.

[*Entering   and taking him by the collar.*] Come
down!   [*She drags him towards the window.*

END OF THE SECOND ACT.

*The Scene is a well-furnished, tastefully-decorated Morn-
ing-room in the house of* ADMIRAL RANKLING. *At
the further end of the room there are two double
doors facing each other, one with glazed panels
opening to a conservatory, the other to a dark room
There are also two doors near to the pillars that
support an archway spanning the room. All is
darkness save for a faint glow from the fire, and
a blue light coming through the conservatory windows.*

PEGGY, *dressed as before, enters quietly, looking about
her.*

PEGGY.

[*In a whisper.*] Where have I got to now, I wonder ? What a dreadful wilderness of a house to wan-
der about in, in the dark, all alone. Oh, for the daylight ! [*Looking at her watch.*] Half-past six. Why,
gracious ! here's a spark of fire ! Oh, joy !

> [*She goes down on her knees, and replenishes
> the fire with coal from the scuttle. The
> door opens, and* GWENDOLINE *peeps in.*

GWENDOLINE.

[*In a whisper.*] What room is this? [*Entering*

noiselessly.] Will the day never break? [*Frightened, and retreating as* PEGGY *makes a noise blowing up the fire.*] Oh!

PEGGY.

[*Frightened.*] Oh! Who is that? [*Looking round.*] Gwendoline!

GWENDOLINE.

Peggy!

PEGGY.

Are you wandering about too?

GWENDOLINE.

Yes. I can't sleep—can you?

PEGGY.

[*Shivering.*] Sleep? No. As if I could sleep in a strange bed in a strange house, in one of Admiral Rankling's night-gowns. You didn't meet any day-light on the stairs, did you?

Another door opens, and ERMYNTRUDE *enters noiselessly.*

GWENDOLINE.

[*Clinging to* PEGGY.] Oh, look there!

ERMYNTRUDE.

[*In a whisper.*] I wonder where I am now.

PEGGY.

Ermyntrude!

ERMYNTRUDE.

[*Clinging to a chair.*] Ah!

PEGGY.

Be quiet! It's we—it's us—it's her and me! Oh, my grammar's going now!

ERMYNTRUDE.

Can't you girls get to sleep?

GWENDOLINE.

I should think not.

PEGGY.

There wasn't any daylight in your room when you came down, was there?

ERMYNTRUDE.

I thought I saw a glimmer through the window on the first floor landing.

PEGGY.

Ah, perhaps that's some of yesterday's. I know! I've made up the fire; let us bivouac here till daybreak. Two by the fire, and take it in turns for the sofa. [*Picking up a bear-skin rug and carrying it to the sofa.*] Who's first for the sofa?

GWENDOLINE.

Ermyntrude.

ERMYNTRUDE.

Gwendoline.

PEGGY.

Come along, Gwendoline. [GWENDOLINE *puts herself upon the sofa, and* PEGGY *covers her with the bearskin.*] There—as soon as you drop off to sleep it will be Ermyntrude's turn. [*Looking through the conservatory doors.*] Oh, how the snow is coming down !

[*Joining* ERMYNTRUDE, *who is warming her hands by the fire. She sits in an arm-chair.*

ERMYNTRUDE.

Peggy—do you know what has become of poor Dinah ?

PEGGY.

Yes, she's locked up upstairs till the morning. Admiral Rankling locked her up.

GWENDOLINE.

[*From the sofa.*] It's a shame !

PEGGY.

Go to sleep ! Oh, what a scene there was ! Admiral Rankling foamed at the mouth. It was lucky they got Mr. Queckett away from him in time.

GWENDOLINE.

[*Sleepily.*] Where is Mr. Queckett ?

PEGGY.

Go to sleep.

ERMYNTRUDE.

[*Leaning against* PEGGY's *knees.*] Mr. Queckett is locked up too, isn't he ?

PEGGY.

Of course he is—till the morning. Miss Dyott locked *him* up—very properly I think.

ERMYNTRUDE.

And where's Miss Dyott?

PEGGY.

Upstairs, in the room next to mine, in hysterics. Hush! I do believe Gwendoline has gone off. Are you pretty comfortable?

ERMYNTRUDE.

[*Her head on* PEGGY's *lap—sleepily.*] Yes, thank you.

PEGGY.

[*Wearily.*] Oh!

> [*The door quietly opens, and* SAUNDERS *appears.* PEGGY *and* ERMYNTRUDE *are hidden from him by the arm-chair.*

SAUNDERS.

[*Sleepily.*] I can't sleep in my room. Where have they put Uncle Jack, I wonder? [*Seeing* GWENDOLINE, *who is sleeping, with the light from the conservatory windows upon her.* Oh—what's that? [*Going softly up to* GWENDOLINE, *and looking at her.*] Why, here's my Gwen. I wonder if she'd mind my sitting near her. [*Turning up his coat collar and sitting gently on the footstool, he leans against the head of the sofa, drowsily.*] Now if any robbers wanted to hurt Gwen, I could kill them. [*Closing his eyes wearily.*] Oh!

> [*Soon there is a sound of heavy regular breathing from the four sleeping figures. The door opens, and* MALLORY *enters.*

MALLORY.

[*Shivering.*] Can't get a blessed wink of sleep. Where have I wandered to? Why, this is the room where the awful row was. [*Seeing* GWENDOLINE.] Hallo, here's one of those school-girls—[*discovering* SAUNDERS]—and—well, this nephew of mine is a devil of a fellow! That isn't a glimmer of fire, surely. [*Walking towards the fireplace, he nearly stumbles over* ERMYNTRUDE.] More girls!

> [*He accidentally knocks over the scuttle. They all wake with a start.*

PEGGY *and* ERMYNTRUDE.

What's that?

GWENDOLINE *and* SAUNDERS.

Who is it?

MALLORY.

Hush, don't be frightened! It's only I.

PEGGY.

Mr. Mallory.

MALLORY.

I've been wandering about—can't sleep.

PEGGY.

No—we can't sleep either.

MALLORY.

Well I don't know about that.

> [ERMYNTRUDE *lights the candle on mantelpiece.*

PEGGY.

Why haven't you and Mr. Saunders gone home? You're not burnt out.

MALLORY.

Perhaps not; but Admiral Rankling asked me to remain, and, if he hadn't, I'm not going to leave this house till my friend Queckett is out of danger.

PEGGY.

Out of danger?

MALLORY.

Yes. Are you aware that you young ladies have brought very grave difficulties upon that unfortunate gentleman?

PEGGY.

[*Crying.*] He encouraged us! He's a man!

MALLORY.

Now, pray don't cry, my dear Miss—what is your name this morning?

PEGGY.

Hesslerigge, and I wish I'd never been born!

MALLORY.

Hesslerigge, and you wish you'd never been born. [*Taking her hand.*] Well, Miss Hesslerigge, the serious aspect of the affair is that Admiral Rankling has a most violent, ungovernable temper.

PEGGY.

[*Tearfully.*] I know. I've never seen a gentleman

foam at the mouth before. It's quite a new experience.

MALLORY.

[*Soothingly.*] Of course—of course—and therefore I'm apprehensive for poor Mr. Queckett's bodily safety. Meanwhile I won't disturb you any longer; come along, Saunders.

PEGGY.

Where are you going?

MALLORY.

To the front door—to speak a word or two of encouragement to that young fellow, Paulover.

PEGGY.

Oh, he is outside still? In the snow!

MALLORY.

Why, he has been walking up and down on the other side of the way all night.

PEGGY.

[*Indignantly.*] And you haven't let him in!

MALLORY.

How could I! You forget that our host has forbidden him the house.

PEGGY.

No, I don't; I saw them roll out into the road together. Girls, shall we open the front door, or shall we remain the mere slaves of etiquette?

GWENDOLINE.

I should like to let him in.

ERMYNTRUDE.

Certainly—why not?

SAUNDERS.

Come along—I know the way.

[SAUNDERS, GWENDOLINE, *and* ERMYNTRUDE
go out quietly.

MALLORY.

[*To* PEGGY.] Well, you'll perhaps pardon my
saying that you are a devil-may-care little school-
girl!

PEGGY.

You make a great mistake. I am not a school-girl;
I am struggling to be a governess.

MALLORY.

Ah, I hope you'll make your way in your pro-
fession.

[PEGGY *has discovered the spirit-stand on the
sideboard and now places it on the table.*

MALLORY.

What are you going to do now?

PEGGY.

Brew poor Mr. Paulover something hot. [*Bringing
the kettle and spirit lamp to the table.*] Light this

lamp for me, please. [*He lights the lamp.*] If you can recommend me at any time to a lady with young daughters I shall be grateful.

MALLORY.

I will—I will.

PEGGY.

I think I am almost capable of finishing any young lady now.

MALLORY.

I am sure you are. [*Looking at the spirit lamp.*] Is that alight? [*They put their heads down close together to look at the lighted lamp.*] That's all right.

PEGGY.

Seems so.   [*They rise and look at one another.*

MALLORY.

We'd better watch it, perhaps, in case it goes out. [*They bob down again with their heads together, and both sit on the same chair.*] You'll get into an awful scrape over your share in last night's business, won't you?

PEGGY.

Frightful; the thought depresses me.

MALLORY.

Do you think Miss Dyott, or Mrs. Queckett, or whatever she is, will send you home?

PEGGY.

She can't—she's got me for ever. She took me, years ago, for a bad debt.

MALLORY.

How can she punish you then?

PEGGY.

I think she will withdraw her confidence from me.

MALLORY.

You won't despair, will you?

PEGGY.

I'll try not to.

MALLORY.

What a jolly little sailor's wife you'd make—brewing grog like this.

PEGGY.

I hope I should do my duty in any station of life to which I might be called.

MALLORY.

I'm a sailor, you know.

PEGGY.

No—are you?

MALLORY.

[*Taking her hand and putting it to his lips.*] You know I am.

PEGGY.

[*Suddenly.*] It's going to boil over! [*They jump*

up quickly, MALLORY *retreats.*] Oh, no, it isn't. [GWENDOLINE *and* ERMYNTRUDE *enter, leading* REGINALD, *with* SAUNDERS *following.* REGINALD *is in a deplorable condition, covered with snow and icicles, his face is white, and his nose red.*] Oh, poor Mr. Paulover!

SAUNDERS.

He's frost-bitten!

PEGGY.

Thaw him by degrees.

> [PEGGY *mixes the grog.* GWENDOLINE *and* ERMYNTRUDE *lead* REGINALD *to a chair before the fire, he uttering some violent but incoherent exclamations.*

ERMYNTRUDE.

He's annoyed with Admiral Rankling.

> [*The girls chafe his hands while he still mutters, with his eyes rolling.*

PEGGY.

It's a good job his language is frozen.

> [*Putting the glass of grog to his lips.*

REGINALD.

[*Reviving.*] Thank you. Take my hat off, please— I bought it from a cabman. [GWENDOLINE *removes his hat, which is very shabby.*] Good morning! Where's my wife Dinah?

PEGGY.

She's quite safe.

REGINALD.

I must see her—speak to her!

PEGGY.

You can't—she's locked up.

REGINALD,

Then I must push a long letter under her door. She *must*, she *shall* know that I am going to walk up and down outside this house all my life! [*Faintly.*] Bring writing materials?

MALLORY.

I'll hunt for the pen and ink.

SAUNDERS.

So will I.

REGINALD.

[*To* PEGGY.] No—no—you do it. These men are bachelors—they can't feel for me!

MALLORY.

Here's a writing-table.

> [PEGGY *runs to* MALLORY *and opens the lid
> of the writing-table.*

PEGGY.

Note-paper and envelopes—where's the—— [*Opening one of the small drawers—she starts back with a cry.*] Oh! [*They all turn and look at her.*

I

ALL.

What's the matter?

PEGGY.

[*Taking from the drawer a large bunch of keys, each with a small label, which she examines breathlessly.*] Duplicate keys of all the rooms in the house! What gross carelessness—to leave keys in an open drawer! Girls, why should not we impress this fact upon Admiral Rankling by releasing Dinah immediately?

GWENDOLINE *and* ERMYNTRUDE.

Oh, yes, yes!

REGINALD.

[*Seizing* PEGGY's *hand.*] Oh, Miss Hesslerigge, my father-in-law is entertaining an angel unawares.

MALLORY.

Oh, stop, stop, stop—I don't think we're quite justified——

REGINALD.

[*Scornfully.*] Hah, I told you he was merely a bachelor! [*pointing to* SAUNDERS.] So is his companion. Give *me* the keys!

PEGGY.

No—no—I take the responsibility of this. I am a girl! [*Going towards the door, and looking at* MALLORY *and* SAUNDERS *as they make way for her.*] I hope you will repent your line of conduct, gentlemen.   [*She goes out.*

MALLORY.

I think we *all* shall.

[*There is a sudden noise, as of some-one fall-
     ing down a couple of stairs.   They start
     and listen.*

GIRLS.

Oh!

MALLORY.

What's that?

ERMYNTRUDE.

[*Looking out at door.*] Here's Admiral Rankling!

[*There is a suppressed exclamation with a
     silent scamper to the further end of the
     room.*

MALLORY.

[*Indignantly.*] What the deuce does a respectable
man want out of bed at this unearthly hour?

RANKLING.

[*In a rage, outside the door.*] Confound that!

GIRLS.

Oh!

REGINALD.

[*Opening the door leading to the dark room.*] Here's
a room here.   Shall we condescend to hide?

ALL.

Yes.

[*They disappear hastily as* RANKLING *appears
     in a dressing-gown, his face pale and his
     eyes red and wild.*

RANKLING.

Hallo! Some one has been sitting up—candles—
and a fire. Ah! [*Sniffing and walking about the room,
he goes straight to the mantelpiece, upon which REGI-
NALD's grog has been left, and takes up the tumbler.*
It's Mallory. [*With suppressed passion.*] It's against
the rules for anybody to sit up in my house! [*Calmly.*]
But I don't mind Mallory—I don't—— [*Looking at
sofa.*] Hallo—Mallory has been turning in here.
[*Going to the sofa and sitting there shaking with
anger.*] Are we never going to have any more daylight? How long am I to wait till that miserable
schoolmistress releases the worm Queckett! Queckett! *Uncle Vere!* The reptile who has made a
fool of me in the eyes of my wife and daughter!
Ugh! But I must husband my strength for Queckett. I have been a very careful man all my life;
as far as muscular economy goes, Queckett shall have
the savings of a lifetime. [*Lying down and pulling
the rug over him.*] Uncle Vere! Ah—I was a wild,
impetuous, daring lad once—[*going to sleep*]—and I
can be unpleasant even now. I can! The Ad-
miralty doesn't know it—Emma doesn't know it—
Queckett shall know it. [*He breathes heavily. The
others have been peeping from their hiding-place, and
as they close the door, PEGGY enters alone, quickly but
silently. She looks for the others, then almost falls
over RANKLING on the sofa, at which she retreats with
a suppressed screech of horror. MALLORY opens the
further door and gesticulates to her violently to be
silent.*

PEGGY.

[*Petrified.*] Oh, my goodness gracious!

[MALLORY *comes and bends over* RANKLING, *listening to his breathing, he then goes to* PEGGY.

MALLORY.

He's dropped off. Where is Mrs. Paulover?

PEGGY.

She's not on that side of the house.

MALLORY.

I've a plan for disposing of the old gentleman. Try the other side.

PEGGY.

I'm going to. [*Turning and clutching* MALLORY.] But, oh, Mr. Mallory, what *do* you think I've done?

MALLORY.

That's impossible to conjecture.

PEGGY.

I've made a mistake about the doors and—I have unlocked Mr. Queckett!

[*She goes out quickly,* MALLORY *thinks for a moment, then bursts into a fit of silent laughter.*

MALLORY.

I love that girl!

REGINALD *appears at the further door, gesticulating.*

REGINALD.

[*In a hoarse whisper.*] Where is my wife? I cannot live longer without her! Where is Dinah!

MALLORY.

Hush! She'll be here in a minute. Come out of there and lend me a hand. [SAUNDERS, GWENDOLINE, *and* ERMYNTRUDE *enter on tiptoe.* *To* REGINALD.] Now then—gently.

> [MALLORY *and* REGINALD *each take an end of the sofa and carry* RANKLING *out through the door into the dark room.*

GWENDOLINE.

[*Breathlessly.*] If they bump him, all's lost!

MALLORY *and* REGINALD *re-appear.*

REGINALD.

I feel warmer now.

MALLORY.

Turn the key.

> [REGINALD *turns the key as* DINAH *and* PEGGY *enter cautiously.*

GWENDOLINE *and* ERMYNTRUDE.

Dinah!

DINAH.

Reggie!

REGINALD.

My wife!

[REGINALD *rushes down to* DINAH *and
embraces her frantically. There is a
general cry of relief as* MALLORY *embraces*
PEGGY, *and* GWENDOLINE *throws her arms
round* SAUNDERS. *Suddenly there is the
sound of some one stumbling downstairs,
accompanied by a smothered exclamation.*

ALL.

[*Listening.*] What's that?

ERMYNTRUDE.

[*Peeping out at the door.*] Here's Uncle Vere got
loose. He has fallen downstairs.

REGINALD.

Oh, bother! Come along, Dinah.

[REGINALD *and* DINAH, SAUNDERS, ERMYN-
TRUDE, *and* GWENDOLINE *go out quickly.*

PEGGY.

[*To* MALLORY.] Rather bad taste of your nephew
and those girls to run after a newly-married couple,
isn't it?

MALLORY.

Yes; *we* won't do it.

PEGGY.

No; but we don't want to be bothered with your
old friend, Queckett, do we?

MALLORY.

No—he's an awful bore. Is the conservatory heated?

PEGGY.

[*Taking his arm.*] I don't mind if it isn't.

> [*They disappear into the conservatory. The door opens, and* QUECKETT, *his face pale and haggard, enters, still wearing his hat and the short covert coat over his evening dress, and carrying his gloves and umbrella.*

QUECKETT.

To whom am I indebted for being let out? Was it by way of treachery, I wonder? Somebody has been sitting up late, or rising early! Who is it? [*Sniffing and looking about him, then going straight to the mantelpiece, taking up the tumbler and smelling the contents.*] I am anxious not to do any one an injustice, but that's Peggy. Oh, what a night I've passed! I have no hesitation in saying that the extremely bad behaviour of Caroline—of the lady I have married—and the ungovernable rage of Rankling, are indelibly impressed upon me. [*Looking round nervously.*] Good gracious! I am actually in the room where Rankling announced his intention of ultimately dislocating my vertebræ. I shall certainly not winter in England. [*The clock strikes seven, he looks at his watch.*] Seven. It will be wise to remain here till the first gleam of daylight, and then leave the house—unostentatiously. I will exchange *no* explanations with Caroline. I shall simply lay the whole circumstances of my injudicious,

boyish marriage before my brother Bob and the other
members of my family. Any allowance which Caroline
may make me shall come through them. [*There is a
sound of something falling and breaking outside the
room.*] The deuce! What's that? [*Going on tiptoe over
to the door, and peeping out.*] Somebody has knocked
something over. [*Snatching up his hat, gloves, and
umbrella.*] I shan't wait till daybreak if they're
breaking other things. [*He hurries to the other door,
opens it, looks out, and closes it quickly.*] People sitting
on the stairs! Is this a plot to surround me? The
conservatory? [*He goes quickly to the conservatory
doors, opens them, then draws back, closing them quickly.*]
Two persons under a palm tree. [*There is a knock at
the door on the right.*] Oh! [*Seeing the door leading
to the dark room.*] Where does that lead to? [*He tries
the door, unlocks it and looks in.*] A dark room! Oh,
I'm so thankful!

> [*He disappears, closing the door after him.
> The knocking outside is repeated, then the
> door opens and* MISS DYOTT *enters. She
> is dressed in her burlesque queen costume,
> her face is pale. She carries the head,
> broken off at the neck, of a terra-cotta bust
> of a woman.*]

MISS DYOTT.

I have broken a bust now. It is an embarrassing
thing to break a bust in the house of comparative
strangers. Oh, will it never be daylight? Does the
milkman *never* come to Portland Place! I have been
listening at the keyhole of Vere's room—not a sound.
He can sleep with the ruin of Volumnia College upon

his conscience while I—— [*Sinking into a chair.*] Ah,
I realise now the correctness of the poet's observation
—" Uneasy lies the head that wears a crown ! "

QUECKETT *comes quietly from the dark room, much
terrified.*

QUECKETT.

Rankling's in there—asleep. In the dark I sat on
him. Oh, what a narrow escape I've had ! [*Coming
behind* MISS DYOTT *and suddenly seeing her.*] Caroline ! Scylla and Charybdis !

[*He bolts back into the dark room.*

MISS DYOTT.

[*Rising alarmed.*] What's that ?

MRS. RANKLING *enters, in a peignoir.*

MRS. RANKLING.

I heard something fall. [*Seeing* MISS DYOTT.]
Mrs. Queckett ! [*Distantly.*] Instructions were given
that everybody should be called at eight. I had
arranged that a more appropriate costume should be
placed at your disposal. [*Seeing the broken bust.*] Ah,
what has happened ?

MISS DYOTT.

I knocked over the pedestal.

MRS. RANKLING.

[*Distressed.*] Oh, bust of myself by Belt ! I saw

him working on it! Oh, Mrs. Queckett, is there no end to the trouble you have brought upon us?

Miss Dyott.

The trouble *you* have brought upon me.

Mrs. Rankling.

What! Why didn't you tell us you had a husband?

Miss Dyott.

Why didn't you tell me that Dinah had a husband?

Mrs. Rankling.

We didn't know it.

Miss Dyott.

Well, if you didn't know your own daughter was married how can you wonder at your ignorance of other people's domestic complications?

Mrs. Rankling.

But that's not all. You have informed us that you are now actually contributing to a nightly entertainment of a volatile description—that you are positively being laughed at in public.

Miss Dyott.

Isn't it better to be laughed at in public, and paid for it, than to be sniggered at privately for nothing!

Mrs. Rankling.

Mrs. Queckett, you are revealing your true character.

Miss Dyott.

It is the same as your own—an undervalued wife. Let me open your eyes as mine are opened. We have engaged to love and to honour two men.

Mrs. Rankling.

I have done nothing of the kind.

Miss Dyott.

I mean one each.

Mrs. Rankling.

Oh—excuse me.

Miss Dyott.

Now—looking at him microscopically—is there much to love and to honour in Admiral Rankling?

Mrs. Rankling.

He is a genial after-dinner speaker.

Miss Dyott.

Hah!

Mrs. Rankling.

It is true he is rather austere.

Miss Dyott.

An austere sailor! All bows abroad and stern at home. Well then—knowing what occurred last night —is there anything to love and to honour in Mr. Queckett?

Mrs. Rankling.

Nothing whatever.

Miss Dyott.

[*Annoyed.*] And yet he is undoubtedly the superior of Admiral Rankling. Very well then—do as I mean to do—put your foot down. If heaven has gifted you with a large one, so much the better.

> [*The voices of* Queckett *and* Rankling *are heard suddenly raised in the adjoining room.*

Rankling.

[*Outside.*] Queckett.

Queckett.

[*Outside.*] My dear Rankling!

Miss Dyott.

Vere !

Mrs. Rankling.

The Admiral has released your husband.

Rankling.

[*In the distance.*] I'll trouble you, sir !

Queckett.

Certainly, Rankling.

Miss Dyott.

[*To* Mrs. Rankling.] Come away, and I will advise you. Bring your head with you.

> [Miss Dyott *and* Mrs. Rankling, *carrying the broken bust, hurry out as* Queckett *enters quickly, followed by* Rankling.

QUECKETT.

Admiral Rankling I shall mark my opinion of your behaviour—through the post.

RANKLING.

Sit down.

QUECKETT.

Thank you   I've been sitting.   I sat on you on the sofa.

RANKLING.

Sit down. [QUECKETT *sits promptly*.] As an old friend of your family, Mr. Queckett, I am going to have a quiet chat with you on family matters.

[RANKLING *wheels the arm-chair near* QUECKETT.

QUECKETT.

[*To himself*.] I don't like his calmness—I don't like his calmness.

[RANKLING *sits bending forward, and glaring at* QUECKETT.

RANKLING.

[*Grimly*.]   How is your sister Janet ?   Quite well, eh ?   [*Fiercely*.]   Tell me—without a moment's delay, sir—how is Janet ?

QUECKETT.

Permit me to say, Admiral Rankling, that whatever your standing with other members of my family, you have *no* acquaintance with the lady you mention.

RANKLING.

Oh, haven't I ?   [*Drawing   his   chair   nearer*

Queckett.] Very well, then. Is *Griffin* quite well—
Finch-Griffin of the Berkshire Royals?

QUECKETT.

I do not know how Major Griffin is, and I feel I
do not care.

RANKLING.

Oh, you don't. Very well, then. [*Drawing his
chair still nearer* QUECKETT.] Will you answer me
one simple but important question?

QUECKETT.

If it be a question a gentleman may answer—
certainly.

RANKLING.

How often do you hear from your brother Tankerville?

QUECKETT.

Oh!

RANKLING.

[*Clutching* QUECKETT's *knee.*] He's Deputy Inspector
of Prisons in British Guiana, you know. Doesn't
have time to write often, does he?

QUECKETT.

Admiral Rankling, you will permit me to remind
you that in families of long standing and complicated
interests there are regrettable estrangements which
should be lightly dealt with. [*Affected.*] You have
recalled memories. [*Rising.*] Excuse me.

RANKLING.

[*Rising.*] No sir, I will not excuse you!

QUECKETT.

Where are my gloves?

RANKLING.

Because, Mr. Queckett, I have your assurance as a gentleman that your brother Tankerville's daughter is married to a charming young fellow of the name of Parkinson. Now I've discovered that Parkinson is really a charming young fellow of the name of Paulover, so that, as Paulover has married my daughter as well as Tankerville's, Paulover must be prosecuted for bigamy, and as you knew that Paulover was Parkinson, and Parkinson Paulover, you connived at the crime, inasmuch as knowing Paulover was Tankerville's daughter's husband you deliberately aided Parkinson in making my child Dinah his wife. But that's not the worst of it!

QUECKETT.

Oh!

RANKLING.

[*Continuing, rapidly and excitedly.*] Because I have since received your gentlemanly assurance that Tankerville's daughter is *my* daughter. Now, either you mean to say that I've behaved like a blackguard to Tankerville—which will be a libel; or that Tankerville has conducted himself with less than common fairness to me—which will be a divorce. And, in either case, without wishing to anticipate the law, I shall personally chastise you, because, although I've been a sailor on the high seas for five and forty years, I have *never* during the whole of that period listened to such a yarn of mendacious fabrications as you spun me last night!

QUECKETT.

[*Beginning to carefully put on his gloves.*] It would be idle to deny that this affair has now assumed its most unpleasant aspect. Admiral Rankling—the time has come for candour on both sides.

RANKLING.

Be quick, sir!

QUECKETT.

I am being quick, Rankling. I admit, with all the rapidity of utterance of which I am capable, that my assurances of last night were founded upon an airy basis.

RANKLING.

In plain words—lies, Mr. Queckett.

QUECKETT.

A habit of preparing election manifestoes for various members of my family may have impaired a fervent admiration for truth, in which I yield to no man.

RANKLING.

[*Advancing in a determined manner.*] Very well, sir!

QUECKETT.

[*Retreating.*] One moment, Rankling. One moment —*if not two!* I glean that you are prepared to assault——

K

RANKLING.

To chastise!

QUECKETT.

Well, to inconvenience a man at whose table you feasted last night. Do so!

RANKLING.

I will do so!

QUECKETT.

I say, do so. But the triumph, when you kneel upon my body—for I am bound to tell you that I shall lie down—the triumph will be mine!

RANKLING.

You are welcome to it, sir. Put down that umbrella!

QUECKETT.

What for?

RANKLING.

I haven't an umbrella.

QUECKETT.

You haven't? Allow me to leave this room, my dear Rankling, and I'll beg your acceptance of this one.

[RANKLING *advances fiercely;* QUECKETT *retreats;* MISS DYOTT *enters.*

QUECKETT.

Caroline!

MISS DYOTT.

Stop, Admiral Rankling, if you please. Any repri-

mand, physical or otherwise, will be administered to
Mr. Queckett at my hands.

QUECKETT.

[*To himself.*] I would have preferred Rankling.
Rankling I could have winded.

> [*He goes out quickly.* MISS DYOTT *following
> in pursuit.*]

MISS DYOTT.

[*As she goes.*] Vere!

RANKLING.

I am in my own house, madam——

> [MRS. RANKLING *enters, carrying the broken
> bust.*

RANKLING.

Emma, go back to bed.

MRS. RANKLING.

Archibald Rankling, attend to me. Don't roll
your eyes—but attend to me.

RANKLING.

Emma, your tone is dictatorial.

MRS. RANKLING.

It is meant to be so, because, after seventeen years
of married life, I am going to speak my mind, at last.
[*Holding up the head before him.*] Archibald, look at
that.

RANKLING.

What's that?

MRS. RANKLING.

Myself—less than ten years ago—the sculptor's earliest effort.

RANKLING.

Broken—made of bad stuff—send it back.

MRS. RANKLING.

It is your memory I wish to send back. Ah, Archibald, do you see how round and plump those cheeks are?

RANKLING.

People alter. You were stout then.

MRS. RANKLING.

I was.

RANKLING.

In those days I was thin.

MRS. RANKLING.

Frightfully.

RANKLING.

Very well, then—the average remains the same. Some day we may return to the old arrangement.

MRS. RANKLING.

If you ever find yourself a spare man again, Archibald, it won't be because I have worried and fretted you with my peevish ill-humour——

RANKLING.

Emma!

Mrs. Rankling.

As you have worried and worn me with yours.

Rankling.

Emma, you have completely lost your head. [*She raises the broken bust.*] I don't mean that confounded bust. That was an ideal.

Mrs. Rankling.

And if a mere sculptor could make your wife an ideal, why shouldn't you try? So, understand me finally, Archibald, I will not be ground down any longer. Unless some arrangement is arrived at for the happiness of dear Dinah and Mr. Paulover, I leave you.

Rankling.

Leave me!

Mrs. Rankling.

This very day.

Rankling.

Wantonly desert your home and husband, Emma?

Mrs. Rankling.

Yes.

Rankling.

[*With emotion.*] And I don't know where to put my hand upon even a necktie!

[*Covering his face with his handkerchief.*

Mrs. Rankling.

All the world shall learn how highly you thought

of Dinah's marriage at Mr. Queckett's party last night.

RANKLING.

[*To himself.*] Oh!

MRS. RANKLING.

And what a very different man you have always been in your own home. [*Beginning to cry.*] And take care, Archibald, that the verdict of posterity is not that you were less a husband and father than a tyrant and oppressor.

[QUECKETT *enters, with* MISS DYOTT *in pursuit; she follows him out.*

MISS DYOTT.

[*As she goes.*] Vere!

[RANKLING *blows his nose and wipes his eyes, and looks at* MRS. RANKLING.

RANKLING.

[*In a conciliatory tone.*] Emma! Emma!

MRS. RANKLING.

[*Weeping.*] Oh, dear, oh, dear!

RANKLING.

Emma. [*Irritably.*] Don't tuck your head under your arm in that way! [*She puts the broken bust on the table.*] Emma—there have been grave faults on both sides. Yours I will endeavour to overlook.

MRS. RANKLING.

Ah, now you are your dear old self again.

RANKLING.

But, Emma, you are occasionally an irritating woman to live with.

MRS. RANKLING.

You are the first who has ever said that.

RANKLING.

So I should hope, Emma.

MRS. RANKLING.

And poor Dinah—you will forgive her?

RANKLING.

On condition that she doesn't see Paulover's face again for five years.

MRS. RANKLING.

Oh, there will be no difficulty about that.

> [REGINALD *and* DINAH *enter; she is dressed for flight.*

DINAH.

Papa!

REGINALD.

My father-in-law!   [*They retreat hastily.*

RANKLING.

[*Madly.*] Who let you out? Who let you in?

[*He goes out after them*—Mrs. Rankling *follows.*

Mrs. Rankling.

[*As she goes out.*] Archibald! continue your dear old self.

[Queckett *enters by another door,* Miss Dyott *following him—both out of breath. They look at each other, recovering themselves.*

Queckett.

I understand that you wish to speak to me, Caroline.

Miss Dyott.

Oh, you—you paltry little man! You mean ungrateful little creature! You laced-up little heap of pompous pauperism! You—you—I cannot adequately describe you. Wretch!

Queckett.

[*Putting on his gloves again.*] Have you finished with me, Caroline?

Miss Dyott.

Finished with you! I shall never have finished with you! Never till you leave me!

Queckett.

[*Rising.*] Till I leave you?

Miss Dyott.

Till you leave me a widow.

QUECKETT.

[*Resuming his seat, disappointed.*] Oh !

MISS DYOTT.

You don't think I expect you to leave me anything else.   Oh, what could I have seen in you !

QUECKETT.

I take it, Caroline, that, in the language of the hunting-field, you " scented " a gentleman.

MISS DYOTT.

Scented a gentleman !   In the few weeks of our marriage I have scented you and cigaretted you, wined you and liqueured you, tailored and hatted and booted you.   I have darned and mended and washed you—gruelled you with a cold, tinctured you with a toothache, and linimented you with the gout. [*Fiercely.*] Have I not ?   Have I not ?

QUECKETT.

You certainly have had exceptional privileges. Familiarity appears to have fulfilled its usual functions and bred——

MISS DYOTT.

The most utter contempt.   Have I not paid your debts ?

QUECKETT.

[*Promptly.*] Not at my suggestion.

MISS DYOTT.

And all for what ?

QUECKETT.

I assume, for Love's dear sake, Carrie.

MISS DYOTT.

For the sake of having the vestal seclusion of Volumnia College telegraphically denominated as Bachelor Diggings!

QUECKETT.

Any collection of young ladies may be so described. The description is happy but harmless. As for the subsequent conflagration——

MISS DYOTT.

Don't talk about it!

QUECKETT.

I say with all sincerity that from the moment the fire broke out till I escaped no one regretted it more than myself. *That* was Tyler!

MISS DYOTT.

Tyler! What Tyler! I make no historical reference when I say what Tyler was it who abruptly tore aside the veil of mystery which had hitherto shrouded the existence of champagne and lobster salad from four young girls! It was you!

QUECKETT.

No, it wasn't, Carrie, upon my word!

MISS DYOTT.

Bah!

QUECKETT.

Upon my honour!

MISS DYOTT.

[*Witheringly.*] Hah!

QUECKETT.

Those vexing pupils played the very devil with me. After you left, the pupils, as it were, dilated.

MISS DYOTT.

Yes, and you ordered them champagne glasses, I suppose! Oh, deceiver!

QUECKETT.

You talk of deception! What about the three o'clock train from Paddington?

MISS DYOTT.

It was the whole truth—there was one.

QUECKETT.

But you didn't travel in it! What about the clergyman's wife at Hereford?

MISS DYOTT.

Go there—you will find several!

QUECKETT.

But you're not staying with them. Oh, Carrie, how can you meet my fearless glance when you recall that my last words yesterday were : " Cabman, drive to Paddington—the lady will pay your fare " ?

Miss Dyott.

I cannot deny that it is by accident you have discovered that I am Queen Honorine in Otto Bernstein's successful comic opera.

Queckett.

And what do you think my family would think of that ?

Miss Dyott.

It is true that the public now know me as Miss Constance Delaporte.

Queckett.

[*Indignantly.*] Oh !   Miss Constance Delaporte !

Miss Dyott.

The new and startling contralto—her first appearance.

Queckett.

And have I, a Queckett, after all, gone and married a Connie ?

Miss Dyott.

You have !   It is true, too, that last night, while you and my pupils were dilating, I was singing—ay, and at one important juncture, dancing !

Queckett.

[*With horror.*] No, no—not dancing !

MISS DYOTT.

Madly, desperately, hysterically, dancing!

QUECKETT.

And to think—if there was any free list—that my brother Bob may have been there.

MISS DYOTT.

But do you guess the one thought that prompted me, buoyed me up, guided my steps, and ultimately produced a lower G of exceptional power.

QUECKETT.

[*With a groan.*] No.

MISS DYOTT.

The thought that every note I sang might bring a bank-note to my lonely Vere at home.

QUECKETT.

Carrie!

MISS DYOTT.

I went through the performance in a dream! The conductor's *bâton* beat nothing but, "Vere, Vere, Vere," into my eyes. Some one applauded me! I thought, "Ah, that's worth a new hat to Vere!" I sang my political verse—a man very properly hissed. "He has smashed Vere's new hat," I murmured. At last came my important solo. I drew a long breath, saw a vision of you reading an old copy of *The Rock* by the fireside at home—and opened my mouth. I remember nothing more till I found myself wildly dancing to the *refrain* of my song. The audience yelled with approbation—I bowed again and again—and then tottered away to sink into the arms of the prompter with the words, "Vere, catch your Carrie"!

QUECKETT.

But my family—my brother Bob——

MISS DYOTT.

What have they ever done for you? While I—it was my ambition to devote every penny of my salary to your little wants.

QUECKETT.

And isn't it?

MISS DYOTT.

No—Vere Albany Bute Queckett; it isn't! The moment I dragged you down that ladder last night, and left behind me the smouldering ruins of Volumnia College, I became an altered woman.

QUECKETT.

Then I will lay the whole affair before my family.

MISS DYOTT.

Do, and tell them to what your selfishness has brought you—that where there was love there is disdain, where there was claret there will be beer, where there were cigars there will be pipes, and where there was Poole there will be Kino!

QUECKETT.

Oh, why didn't I wait and marry a lady?

Miss Dyott.

You *did* marry a lady! But scratch the lady and you find a hardworking comic actress!

Queckett.

Be silent, madam!

Miss Dyott.

Ha! Ha! This is my revenge, Vere Queckett! To-night I will dance more wildly, more demonstratively than ever!

Queckett.

I forbid it!

Miss Dyott.

You forbid it! *You* dictate to Constance Delaporte—the hit of the opera! I am Queen Honorine? [*She slaps her hands and sings with great abandonment, and in the pronounced manner of the buffo queen, the song she is supposed to sing in* Bernstein's *opera. Singing.*]

> 'Rine, 'Rine, Honorine!
> Mighty, whether wife or queen;
> Firmer ruler never seen,
> Than 'Rine, 'Rine? *La!*

Queckett.

[*Indignantly.*] I will write to my married sisters!

Miss Dyott.

Do—and I will call upon them! [*Singing.*]

Man's a boasting, fretting fumer,
Smoking alcohol consumer,
Quick of temper, ill of humour!

QUECKETT.

Oh, you shall sing this to my family!

MISS DYOTT.

I will!   [*Singing with her hands upon her hips.*]

Woman has no petty vices,
Cuts her sins in good thick slices,
With a smile that sweet and nice is!

QUECKETT.

[*Writhing.*] Oh!

MISS DYOTT.

[*Boisterously.*] Refrain!   [*Singing and dancing.*]

'Rine, 'Rine, Honorine!
Mighty, whether wife or queen,
Firmer ruler never seen,
Than 'Rine, 'Rine! *La!*

[*With a burst of hysterical laughter she sinks
into a chair.*

QUECKETT.

Oh, I will tell my brother of you!

[*Daylight appears through the conservatory
doors.   MRS. RANKLING and DINAH
enter.   MALLORY and PEGGY enter from
conservatory, " spooning."*]

Mrs. Rankling.

My dear Mrs. Queckett, I owe everything to you
—my treatment of the dear Admiral has had won-
derful results. What do you think! The Admiral
and Mr. Paulover are quite reconciled and understand each other perfectly. [Rankling *and* Paulover
*enter, glaring at each other and quarrelling violently in
undertones.*] Look—the Admiral already regards him
as his own child.

[Saunders, Ermyntrude, *and* Gwendoline
enter and join Peggy *and* Mallory.

Dinah.

[*Sobbing.*] But we are to be separated for five
years. Oh, Reggie, you trust me implicitly, don't
you ?

Reginald.

[*Fiercely.*] I do. And that is why I warn you
never to let me hear of you addressing another
man.

Dinah.

Oh, Reggie !   [*They embrace.*

Rankling.

Don't do that! You don't see me behaving in
that way to Mrs. Rankling—and we've been married
for years.

Mrs. Rankling.

[*To* Dinah.] But you and Mr. Paulover are to be
allowed to meet once every quarter.

Reginald.

Yes—in the presence of Admiral Rankling and a
policeman !

L

[Mrs. Rankling, Rankling, Dinah *and* Reginald *join the others.* Otto Bernstein *enters quickly and excitedly, carrying a quantity of newspapers.*

Bernstein.

I beg your pardon. I must see Miss Constance Delaporte—I mean, Miss Dyott.

Miss Dyott.

Mr. Bernstein.

Bernstein.

Your house is burnt down. It does not madder. You have made a gread hit in my new oratorio—I mean my gomic opera. I have been walking up and down Fleet Street waiting for the babers to gome out. [*Handing round all the newspapers.*] Der "Dimes" —Der "Delegraph"—Der "Daily News"—Der "Standard"—Der "Bost"—Der "Ghronicle"! Dey are all gomplimentary except one, and dat I gave to the gabman.

Miss Dyott.

[*Reading.*] "Miss Delaporte—a decided acquisition."

Bernstein.

Go on!

Queckett.

[*Reading.*] "Miss Delaporte—an imposing figure." [*Indignantly.*] What do they know about it?

Bernstein.

[*Excitedly.*] Go on! Go on! I always say I do

not read the babers, but I *do!* [*To* Miss Dyott.]
You will get fifty bounds a week in my next oratorio
— I mean, my gomic opera.

QUECKETT.

Fifty pounds a week! My Carrie! I shall be
able to snap my fingers at my damn family.

Mrs. Rankling.

How very pleasing! [*Reading.*] "A voice of great
purity, a correct intonation, and a lower G of decided
volume, rendered attractive some music not remarkable for grace or originality."

[BERNSTEIN *takes the paper from* Mrs.
Rankling.

Bernstein.

I did not see dat—I will give *dat* to the gabman.
Goo-bye—I cannot stay. I am going to have a
Turkish bath till the evening babers gome out. I
always say I do not read the evening babers—but I
do! [*He bustles out.*

Mrs. Rankling.

Mrs. Queckett, I shall book stalls at once to hear
your singing.

Rankling.

No, Emma—dress circle.

Mrs. Rankling.

Stalls, Archibald.

RANKLING.

[*Glaring.*] Dress circle !

MRS. RANKLING.

Stalls, Archibald, or I leave you for ever !

RANKLING.

[*Mildly.*] Very well, Emma. I have no desire but to please you.

QUECKETT.

I take this as a great compliment, my dear Rankling. Carrie and I thank you. But I can't hear of it. I insist on offering you both a seat in my box.

MISS DYOTT.

Your box !

QUECKETT.

[*Softly to her.*] Hush ! Carrie, my darling ! Your Vere's private box !

MISS DYOTT.

Mr. Queckett's private box, during my absence at night, will be our lodgings, where he will remain under lock and key. [PEGGY *laughs at* QUECKETT.

QUECKETT.

[*To* PEGGY.] Oh, you vexing girl !

MALLORY.

[*Annoyed.*] Excuse me, my dear Queckett but while looking at the plants in the conservatory, I became engaged to Miss Hesslerigge.

[*There is a general exclamation of surprise.*

REGINALD.

[*To* MALLORY.] Ah, coward, you haven't to wait five years!

JANE enters.

JANE.

Oh, if you please ma'am, Tyler——

MISS DYOTT, QUECKETT, PEGGY, *and* DINAH.

Tyler!

JANE.

Tyler wants to know who is to pay him the reward for being the first to fetch the fire engines last night?

QUECKETT.

I will!

MISS DYOTT.

No—I will. Tyler has rendered me a signal service. He has demolished Volumnia College. From the ashes of that establishment rises the Phœnix of my new career. Miss Dyott is extinct—Miss Delaporte is alive, and, during the evening, kicking. I hope none will regret the change—I shall not, for one, while the generous public allow me to remain a Favourite!

THE END.

Printed by BALLANTYNE, HANSON & CO.
London and Edinburgh.